# PRINCE
# AT BLACK PONY INN

D1096391

# PRINCE
# AT BLACK PONY INN

## Christine
## Pullein-Thompson

RAVETTE BOOKS

This edition published by Ravette Books Limited 1989

Phototypeset by Input Typesetting Ltd, London
Printed and bound in Great Britain
for Ravette Books Limited,
3 Glenside Estate, Star Road,
Partridge Green, Horsham,
West Sussex RH13 8RA
by Cox & Wyman Ltd,
Reading

ISBN 1 85304 229 3

# One
# A bucking broncho

It was December and the first day of the holidays. We were all in the stable yard staring at our newest arrival, a liver chestnut gelding of fifteen hands called Hillingdon Prince, but nicknamed Broncho. Usually we take human guests at our Black Pony Inn, but he was decidedly equine and our greatest challenge yet. My brother Ben was there, tall, fair-haired with broad shoulders and brown eyes. He is older than me, but younger than my elder brother James. Lisa, my younger sister, was also there. She is small for her age with a thin face and a determined chin and she never takes no for an answer. Broncho's owner, Mrs Nuttal, was small and wispy with the lined look of a woman who has given her life to horses.

"Are you putting him in tonight?" she asked.

"We would rather he went out," replied Ben.

"You won't catch him then. It took three of us five hours to catch him yesterday," she replied.

"Thanks for telling us," I replied without meaning to sound sarcastic.

"We'll manage somehow," said Ben.

Broncho's owner was going now, starting up her horse box, looking ageless and fearless and completely without vanity.

Ben was holding Broncho. He was a beautiful horse with breeding written all over him, with an eye which had fire, superiority, fearlessness and pure devilment in it, evenly mixed. His head had an Arab look about it, and his legs were fine with short cannon bones, which looked as strong as steel. His shoulder sloped, his chest was wide, his girth deep, his quarters strong and muscular, his back short and straight. He was the sort of horse you dream about, and he had come to us as unrideable – we were the last hope, all that stood between him and the humane killer.

I touched his shoulder and he flinched. I touched his neck and he tossed his head. He was as tense as a balloon about to burst.

"Don't touch him. Leave him alone," cried Ben.

"He's mad," cried Mummy. "I forbid you to get on him, absolutely, and that's final." But she knew her words were empty words, without meaning for us. We had accepted the challenge weeks ago when we had written back to his owner saying that we would have him. There was no going back.

"Let's put him out," Ben said. "We'll catch him somehow. If we leave him in, he'll go mad."

"Your necks are more important than

money," cried Mummy. "Why did you take him on?"

"Because we like to be tried and tested," answered my brother. "And because we are going to succeed and earn the bonus Miss Nuttal offered us . . ."

"That's right," I cried. "We need the money."

We always needed money. It was like a disease in our family, which we all suffered from – a chronic incurable shortage of money. And we had expensive tastes. We liked hunting, and going to shows, and Pony Club camp and keeping a horse each, and one to spare. And Mummy and Dad liked good food and dinner by candlelight and living in the large house, which Dad had bought in our better-off days.

"He's lovely," said Lisa, speaking for the first time. "But he looks so wild, as though he'll never be tamed, as though he doesn't want to be, as though he despises us all, and is greater than any of us. I wish he had never come."

"Don't be stupid," I snapped, though half of me felt the same, while the other half was full of hope, and a fantastic dream of success.

We turned him into the smallest of our paddocks and he galloped round it like a wild mustang, his tail arched above his back. Then he stood on his hind legs, before reeling round to give a display of bucking, which made us all gasp.

"You'll never stay on that," cried Mummy.

"Not in a month of Sundays," cried Lisa.

I began to feel weak at the knees, but Ben said, "Of course we will. Don't be silly. Sitting on that little display is no more difficult than riding across country over a testing course. Anyway, we'll lunge him tomorrow and get the bucks out of him. We're not crazy, not yet anyway."

It was nearly dark now with a raw, biting feeling in the air, and a crispness which meant frost. Ben and I fetched hay for our new horse while everyone else disappeared indoors to get tea. He wouldn't come near us. He looked like a horse in a western, fresh off the prairie; he smelt the air and stamped with his hoofs and I said, "I think we're going to be defeated, Ben. I feel it in my bones."

Welcoming lights shone out from the house. Mrs Mills, our oldest lodger, opened the back door to call, "Tea."

Our own horses were already settled in their loose boxes for the night, their teeth munching hay steadily, their eyes quiet and contented.

"We're going to have a fight," said Ben walking towards the house. "And I love a fight."

"Either we win and he's broken, or we're broken," I answered.

"We'll take it slowly, make friends, win his confidence," Ben said.

"If he had come from a bad home, it might be easy. But Mrs Nuttal knows about horses, she loves them. Why should we succeed when she didn't?" I asked.

And Ben gave no answer.

We walked into the house comfortable in our riding clothes after a week of school uniform.

"We've got to succeed," said my brother, "because our reputation is at stake. If we win, more horses will follow. We will be considered experts and experts have a habit of growing rich, and I want to be rich. I want to wear breeches made by the Queen's tailor, and boots to measure."

"You're mad," I answered. "Clothes don't matter. It's what you *are* that counts."

We poured ourselves mugs of tea in our old-fashioned kitchen which I love. Mummy still looked worried. Mrs Mills was knitting socks for us, sitting on a chair by the Aga cooker. Twinkle, our cat, was keeping warm by the simmering oven, while Lisa was playing Monopoly by herself on the floor. There were Christmas cards hanging from the ceiling.

"We'll make friends with him tomorrow," said Ben. "We'll make him love us, Harriet, trust us. We won't ride him until he does. It's the only way."

Ben was walking up and down the kitchen now, his eyes alight with excitement. I saw myself on Broncho, cantering a perfect circle. It'll take time, I thought. But the best things in life take time and, when we've finished, we'll be famous. And it seemed quite easy then, just a short, hard struggle and then victory, like embarking on a long walk and knowing you can make it with a bit of an extra effort – that it's possible. I never imagined at that moment the heartache, frenzy and anxiety which lay ahead; nor the tears I would shed, nor the sleepless nights I would endure, all for one beautiful horse, and because of a letter we had recklessly answered at the end of the summer.

Lisa continued playing Monopoly with great concentration. She is clever, obstinate, brave and infuriating in almost equal parts. Ben ate five fairy cakes without noticing what he was eating.

Mummy said, "If you break your necks I shall commit suicide."

Then Dad came in, fresh from the job he hated, to complain about the telephone bill. And now there was a moon lighting up the stables, making everything look like fairyland outside. And I thought, the ground will be rock hard tomorrow, so we won't be able to ride and if it continues cold for a month the holidays will be over, and we won't have ridden Broncho at all. What then?

"Why do you all always collect in here?" asked Mummy. "There's three sitting rooms. How can I get dinner with you all here?"

"It's because of you. We love you," replied Lisa. "We want to be near you."

"I don't care. Scram!" cried Mummy. "Clear off! Play your game on a table like a

10

human being. And stop eating cakes, Ben. You won't want any dinner."

It was like any other day and yet it was a beginning of a part of our lives we would never forget. The next few weeks were to change us, leave us harder but more wary. They were going to test us as we had never been tested before. But we didn't know that then. Ben was full of jokes and bravado and went whistling upstairs, while I sat down to read a book called *Breaking and Schooling From A-Z* by George Hammerson, late instructor at the World's Equitation Centre, New England, while outside the ground froze harder and harder and Broncho stood alone in his paddock, aloof and untamed, beautiful beyond words.

# Two
# A horse in a thousand

The ground was white with frost in the morning, the water troughs covered with ice thicker than the thickest glass.

"If only we had an indoor school," grumbled Ben, thawing out the yard tap with the house kettle.

"Or even an outdoor one," I replied.

"We had better spread the midden in the smallest paddock and lunge him on that."

I didn't need to ask who "him" was for Broncho seemed to dominate everything. He was like one of those people who changes the atmosphere of a room when he enters, who makes heads turn automatically, who dominates a party.

We could sense his presence as we went about our chores, watching us, measuring us up. And it wasn't a nice feeling. It was rather frightening, in a strange, uncanny way.

"I think he's lived before," I said to Ben. "I think he really was a prince."

"More likely a dictator," Ben replied.

We couldn't get near him. We simply broke the ice and threw him a wad of hay while he watched us from a distance, ears upright, eyes wary.

"We'll be stronger after breakfast," said Ben. "Let's eat lots and then tackle him. We can drive him into a corner. There's enough of us . . ."

"And we're stronger than poor Jean Nuttal," I added.

We ate eggs for breakfast and huge helpings of cereals.

"How is he?" asked Mummy.

"Still alive," replied Ben.

"Have you caught him yet?"

"We haven't tried."

"Do be careful."

"We will. I promise," I said.

"I'll wear the cross-country helmet when I ride him for the first time," announced Ben.

"Why should you ride him first?" I asked.

"Because I'm bigger and stronger," he answered.

"Yes, let him," said Mummy.

"We have to catch him first," I muttered.

Ten minutes later we approached him with a bowl of oats and halters hidden behind our backs. He wasn't interested. He looked rather bored and simply walked away.

"He's summed us up," said Ben after a time. "We had better get James and Lisa."

"And do what?" I asked.

"Drive him into a corner."

"Supposing he goes mad when he's been cornered?" I asked.

"Oh don't be stupid," snapped Ben. "What's the matter with you?"

"I don't know. I just wish he was like

Lorraine," I answered. Lorraine is my own grey mare and in my eyes entirely perfect.

"If he was like Lorraine, he wouldn't be here," replied Ben, starting to call, "Lisa, James. Come here, we need you."

"They won't hear," I said; but presently they came, pulling on boots and gloves, asking, "What is it now?" James had a mug of half-drunk coffee in one hand.

"You won't need that; we are going to corner him," said Ben, pointing at the coffee mug.

"Corner what?"

"Broncho, of course."

"You know I hate horses," said James.

"We'll give you a rake off when we're paid," I replied.

"If you *are* paid," answered James, putting his coffee mug on an upturned bucket.

We walked slowly towards Broncho, our arms outstretched. He watched us calmly, as though he had seen it all before. Then he started to walk towards the corner of the paddock nearest the stables with a knowing look in his eye.

"He's going to give in," said Ben. "I can see it on his face. He knows he's beaten."

But as he neared his corner, he started to trot. "He's going to make a break. Stand firm," cried Ben.

Lisa began running. Cassie neighed from her loose box, her eyes alight with admiration. Broncho lengthened his stride and sailed over the rail fence as though it was a mere two foot high instead of four feet six.

"Run for the yard gate!" screamed Ben.

Lisa slammed the yard gate shut, while Broncho's hoofs pounded across the frozen lawn and Ben ran towards the front gates. Then Broncho's hoofs churned up the freezing strawberries and pounded across the last of the leeks. Our paying guest, Colonel Hunter, appeared, clutching *The Times*.

"He's ruining the garden," he shouted, as though we didn't know!

"He's on *my* strawberries," cried Mrs Mills, tiny in woolly cap, checked coat and bedroom slippers.

We'll never catch him now, I thought. He'll have to live in the garden and Dad will be furious.

Ben had closed the front gates now which are wrought iron and rather majestic.

"What a devil," he shouted, rubbing his hands together. "Let's drive him into the yard."

"Supposing he jumps the yard gate and disappears?" I asked.

"He can't. It's six feet high," replied Ben. "But Lisa, you'll guard it, won't you? Just in case."

"Supposing he jumps Lisa too?" I asked.

"Do shut up," said Ben.

"And hurry up," cried James. "It's freezing and I need more coffee."

Broncho pounded round the garden three times before he eventually entered the yard,

15

his head high, his nostrils snorting, while Cassie went wild in her box with delight. We tried to corner him, but he defeated us every time, brooms went flying, the bucket with James's coffee on it was kicked to smithereens, while James stood crying, "My coffee, my coffee!" in mock dismay.

"It was *my* mug," cried Lisa. "It had an Easter Egg in it last Easter, don't you remember? Mrs Mills gave it to me. Why do you always take my things? I hate you James."

"Shut up," yelled Ben.

Broncho was on the lawn again now, watching us with glee in his eyes.

"He's enjoying himself," said Lisa bitterly. "I can see it on his miserable face."

"We'll chase him into the paddock," shouted Ben. "Come on."

We opened the gate. Snow was falling now like powdered soap from a leaden sky. It will grow thicker soon, I thought. We're in for a white Christmas.

He went into the paddock quite easily and turned round to snort at us in triumph.

"We'll have to starve him out," said Ben. "It's the only way."

"He'll jump the fence again," cried James over his shoulder, already running towards the house. "He'll keep going round and round the garden. You had better send him back."

"He'll ruin Christmas. I hate him. He looks so superior. Look at his face now. He knows he's beaten us," said Lisa, her nose running. "My hands are freezing."

"No more food until you're caught. Do you understand?" shouted Ben. "It's cruel to be kind. You've got to give in; otherwise it's the abattoir for you."

"Why couldn't he be ugly?" I asked. "He doesn't even look mean. He looks brave – a horse in a thousand."

"That's why we must succeed," replied Ben.

"But it's cruel not to feed him," I answered.

"He's clever," said Ben, "he'll know when he's beaten. He won't starve."

"If only it was summer," I said.

The snow was falling faster and thicker now. Ben's fair hair was coated with it, and the woolly gloves I was wearing were soaked through.

"If only there wasn't a time limit. If only we had months instead of weeks to break him," I continued.

"If only, if only. Why can't you forget 'if only'?" snapped Ben.

It snowed all afternoon. Broncho looked miserable but unbeaten. We offered him food from a bucket but he refused to come near. And now he wouldn't look at us. He stared into the distance as though there lay a happier land over the horizon with green pastures and no humans to bother him; or maybe he wouldn't look for fear of being tempted. We couldn't tell. I had never left a horse without food before. It made me sad inside and I knew that I would lie awake half the night worrying about him.

We shut all the gates before we went indoors. Broncho was standing, resting a leg in the far corner of the field now, still staring into the distance, his mane soaked through with melted snow. We walked in slowly.

"It's our only hope," said Ben. "Perhaps tomorrow he'll give in."

"We can give him a warm mash then and a great pile of hay," I suggested.

"Not too much. He must stay hungry if we're to catch him again," replied Ben quickly.

"I feel cruel," I said. "If it wasn't snowing, I wouldn't mind so much."

"He'll give in all the sooner because of the snow," replied Ben.

"Have you caught him?" shouted Mrs Mills the minute we entered the kitchen.

"Not yet," replied Ben.

"Is he still in the garden?"

"No," I said.

I was miserable all evening because of Broncho. Later the snow stopped falling and there was a pale moon in a dreamy night sky, and I could see Broncho standing in the same corner as he had been most of the day, resting a leg, his mane all frosted, but his eyes still alert. What is he thinking? I wondered. Is he making plans? Or dreaming of his youth? What do horses think about when they stand up all night long, hungry and alone in an empty paddock?

I went to bed early and dreamed that Broncho was galloping round London, dodging the traffic until at last he met a bus full on and lay with broken legs, while a crowd collected and two strong policemen took me away in a police car.

When I got up, Broncho was standing in the same corner of the paddock, his belly line run up like a greyhound's. The landscape was sprinkled with snow, with the ground rock hard underneath. The sky was a cold grey with no promise of sunshine in it. I dressed quickly and put some oats in my pocket and approached Broncho, talking to him all the time saying, "Come on, I'm not going to hurt you. I'm your friend. You needn't be afraid."

But I knew that he wasn't afraid. He never had been. He just didn't want to be a slave for the rest of his life. I knew how he felt. He was too clever to be a horse, to accept a horse's life without question. He had broken the ice in his trough with a hoof, but it was nearly empty, so soon he would be thirsty too.

I looked at his proud head and wondered how long it would take him to give in. I imagined him starving to death. I said, "Please give in Broncho, please." But he simply looked away like someone who doesn't want to know you.

"All right, have it your own way," I said then. "Starve to death. Don't you know we all have to work? You can't have oats and hay and not work. It's the same for all of us.

We would all like life to be one long holiday. But it can't be. Can't you accept that?"

Hearing the anger in my voice, he started to trot in a small circle snorting and blowing, as though trying to say, "I'm not giving in."

"Have it your own way then," I shouted. "Starve to death."

I left the paddock, slamming the yard gate after me and the snow started to fall again. From the kitchen came the sound of Lisa and Ben shouting at one another. And I thought, we've made another mistake, and all for the sake of money; there won't be any riding these holidays anyway, the weather isn't good enough.

Then Ben appeared crying, "Any luck?" And I answered rudely, "Of course not, you fool. He's far too clever for us."

And Ben asked, "Did you really expect to succeed in twenty-four hours? You must be mad."

And I knew he was right, that we couldn't expect breaking Broncho to be easy. That it had to be long and hard.

"It will take time but we'll win,' said Ben. "He's looking less confident already. He's a tough nut and you can only crack them with tough nutcrackers; there's no other way."

"And we're the nutcrackers?" I said.

Ben nodded. "And supposing we break?" I asked.

"Nutcrackers don't break," replied Ben.

# Three
# "I'll wear the crash helmet"

The next day was the same, only worse, because now I couldn't look at Broncho without feeling cruel. He had hardly any stomach on him now, and it went right in where the hair parted on his flank. Poverty marks had appeared, and his neck looked thin and droopy and his hoofs were full of snow. A lump rose in my throat when I looked at him. I said, "Can't we give in? Supposing he gets colic or gets really ill standing out in the cold with nothing inside him?" And there was only solid ice in his trough now.

"Just another twenty-four hours," pleaded Ben. "And then we can telephone Jean Nuttal and admit defeat, and Roy can come with his humane killer, and bang, bang, it will be all over."

"He looks so pitiful," I said.

"It's no worse than war. Ask Colonel Hunter about wars. He'll tell you about the trenches in the 1914–18 war; he's never forgotten the mud, and the horses lying half dead with their quarters shot away. And the rats gnawing at . . ."

"Shut up," I screamed, my hands over my ears.

"We are being cruel to be kind," bellowed Ben.

"Two wrongs don't make a right," I yelled.

"It's always darkest before dawn," quoted Ben. "He's looking at us. Look Harriet." It was true. He wasn't looking into the distance any more but staring at us with clear, courageous eyes, which I thought held respect in them.

"Let's give him some water," said Ben. "We can stand by the trough while he drinks."

We fetched a bucketful and poured it in. He approached gingerly, and drank with his nose outstretched. Ben touched his mane and he moved away, but calmly and quietly, as though the human hand simply annoyed him a little.

"We're winning," said Ben.

"We hope," I added.

Our own horses needed exercising. We rode them out, riding one, leading another across the frozen landscape, our hands and feet freezing, while they slipped and slid and the snow blew in our faces.

"We had better cut their oats altogether," said Ben. "We don't want any azatoria."

"They are not very fit," I answered.

"But it's still possible," said Ben.

Broncho was looking over the fence when we returned. "I think he's come to a decision," said Ben. "I think he's changed his mind."

I had the same feeling. He was looking at everything with interest now; as though he might yet take part in it. He was no longer staring at us from the outside, he was coming inside our lives to join us.

"We'll catch him after lunch," said Ben. "I knew he was clever. He's worked it out, he understands. We must treat him as though he's clever. It's no good treating him as though he's a normal horse."

And now we were excited. It was as though we were suddenly capable of clearing the first obstacle in a long line of jumps, each one growing higher. We thought we had found the key to Broncho's character. That one step would lead to another. Ben started to whistle and I said, "He will be marvellous to ride. He'll learn everything so quickly with his sort of brain."

"And just think of riding him across country," exclaimed Ben. "Wow!"

"I wish it was tomorrow already. That he was already caught and tamed," I said.

We stayed indoors for a long time after lunch watching the snow falling. Ben fell asleep with a book in his hand, while James paced the kitchen, saying, "I can't stand college for another term. I can't stay there another two years . . ." And Mummy looked distracted while Lisa sat next door watching television. At three o'clock I wakened Ben and we wrapped ourselves up in thick mufflers and our warmest coats and fed our own horses, because we wanted Broncho to see that "good" horses have lots of food while "bad" horses have nothing. He watched us over the fence with snow-crusted mane and hoofs washed pale by the snow. His star looked off-white on his forehead against the whiteness of the snow, and the trees were bowed under the weight of it, and the flowers were buried. And the house looked smaller thatched by snow, and everything seemed much stiller and somehow muted, and older – far, far older.

When we had fed our own horses, we approached Broncho with oats in a bucket and he walked up to us and gave Ben a familiar nudge, as if to say, "All right, you win."

I gave Ben a rope to attach to the head-collar we had left on him, and he followed us into a loose-box. We fetched him water and hay and then, very slowly, we put a rug on him with straw underneath.

And now we hardly dared to breathe for fear of upsetting him. Then we bolted his door top and bottom and rushed into the house screaming, "He's caught. He's in a box, he's given in."

And Ben started to dance round the kitchen crying, "Think of all that lovely money – thirty pounds a week, wasn't it, and a bonus of two hundred if we succeed. What shall we spend it on?"

"Don't count your chickens before they are hatched," said Mummy from behind the washing machine.

But Ben wouldn't stop. "A black hunting coat for you, Harriet," he cried. "And mahogany-topped hunting boots for me. Or a dinner jacket. How about a dinner jacket? How would I look in a dinner jacket?"

"Why not a saddle each?" I asked. "A jumping saddle; a plastic one for you because it won't need much cleaning, and a leather one for me?"

After a time I went upstairs and stared out of the passage window. Broncho was looking out of his box, his eyes shining and he didn't look as though he had suffered a defeat; he looked pleased with himself, confident. Cassie was leaning out of her box trying to touch his nose and it wasn't snowing any more. Everything looked clean and peaceful and I suddenly remembered that there were only a few days left until Christmas, and I hadn't bought Mummy a present.

The next day we put a saddle on Broncho and he shook all over like a leaf in a wind and cowered in one corner of his box. I gave him bits of bread and talked to him, but he went on trembling, and Ben said, "We had better leave it on him, let's tie him up. He's got to get used to it."

So we tied him to the ring on the manger and left him trembling, his quarters hunched under him, his eyes wild. And we both knew it was a setback to our hopes, though we didn't say so. "He really is afraid now," said Ben.

"Exactly," I agreed. "He's terrified. I wonder why?"

"Your guess is as good as mine," replied Ben.

We spent the rest of the morning carting the midden to the smallest of the paddocks, so that we could ride on it. And after a time, our arms started to ache, and we were so hot we took off our coats.

"Where's Lisa. Why doesn't she help?" cried Ben. "She'll ride on it as soon as it's finished for certain."

"There's only two wheelbarrows, and she's much slower than us," I answered.

We kept slipping on frozen snow and our clothes started to smell and then, at last, it was lunchtime. Broncho was still shaking, so we took off his saddle, talking to him all the time. "There must be some reason for his fear," I said.

"I think he's pretending," answered Ben, walking towards the house.

"I don't agree," I said. Dad was home and made us change our trousers before lunch.

James had been tobogganing with friends and was ruddy-faced and cheerful and Lisa was warm from reading all morning with Twinkle on her lap. Mrs Mills had been for a walk and kept shouting about the snow and how deep it was on the common and Colonel Hunter started to remember the Himalayas in 1925 when Britain owned India.

Afterwards we decided to exercise Lorraine and Ben's Welsh cob Solitaire and we turned the others out to exercise themselves, all except Broncho who rushed round and round his box like a lunatic.

"He's getting exercise anyway," said Ben as we set off across the common.

Our mounts made hoofmarks in the untouched snow and the sky was now an endless blue. We walked and jogged and there was a wind which stung our faces and soon we turned homewards again.

"Let's lunge Broncho tomorrow in a full set of tack," suggested Ben. "He can buck to his heart's content then."

"And he needs exercise," I agreed.

"We'll lunge him for ages," said Ben. "And the next day we'll lead him out off a horse for miles and miles. And the next day we'll ride him."

"If the weather allows," I answered.

"The roads are clear now," replied Ben. "And we must have a target. One never gets anywhere without a deadline."

"I think we should take our time," I answered.

But Ben wouldn't listen. Like Lisa, he hated waiting for anything. He wanted money and success and fame, all at once before he was any older. We were all tired of being poor, of watching other pupils at school boasting of mopeds and new bicycles, of holidays in Spain and TVs in their bedrooms. They gave the teachers end-of-term presents which cost a fortune and went to the cinema every week, and bought make-up and had their hair cut at the most expensive shop in the area. And Ben wanted all those things too. So we hurried home and settled the horses for the night, and Broncho nudged us over his box door like an old friend, his liver chestnut coat gleaming, his eyes sparkling.

"We've won one battle already, can't you see?" cried Ben. "He trusts us . . . !"

"Touch wood," I cried, grabbing the loose-box door.

"It's all in his mind. He's accepted us now as superior beings," said Ben with frightening self-confidence.

"I wish the weather would change. If we fall on this ground, it will really hurt," I said.

"We're not going to fall," replied Ben.

When Lorraine was rugged up for the night, I joined Broncho in his box. "We're your friends," I told him. "Really, truly."

He smelt my hair and pushed me with his nose. He was calm and friendly, but I had the feeling that he was keeping his options open, that he was fully independent with a mind of his own, because he was himself a leader who wouldn't want to be led. "Be nice to us," I pleaded. "Please."

I followed Ben into the house, thinking. "He's making it sound too easy, nothing in life is that easy."

And I dreamed that night that Broncho was galloping with Ben along a long, long road, while I followed on Lorraine, calling, "Stop, please, stop."

Next morning everything was dripping and the air was warm. We tacked up Broncho and lunged him and he looked at us with confidence and did everything he was told.

28

We lunged him at the walk and trot, first on one rein and then on another and it was obvious that he had been lunged many times before.

"Let's ride him after an early lunch," said Ben.

"Isn't it a bit soon?"

"I'm not scared, and he isn't, just look at him!" cried Ben. "After all, he's been here four days. It's ridiculous how little we've done."

"I think we should wait."

"Well, I don't," answered Ben. And as usual he won. I was filled with misgivings all through lunch. Ben had sworn me to secrecy. "You know how Mummy is – nothing but nerves. I'll wear the crash helmet. We can lead him for a few miles first, exhaust him, then I'll get on," he said. "You lead him to begin with and I'll follow on my bike."

"The weather's changed," shouted Mrs Mills, who is deaf. "You would never think there was a drought back in the summer, would you?"

"No," I shouted back.

"When can I have a moped?" asked James. "I'm seventeen, and all my friends have mopeds."

"You'll kill yourself on a moped," replied Mummy.

"My friends haven't. Why can't I have a moped for Christmas?" asked James, sounding like a three-year-old.

And I realized that tomorrow was

Christmas Eve and I *still* hadn't bought Mummy's present.

"Let's leave Broncho in today. I need to go shopping," I said.

"We can't. He needs exercising. We can't leave him cooped up in his box day after day. He'll go mad," replied Ben.

"How is he?" asked Mummy.

"Marvellous, super, a reformed character," said Ben.

"I shall be dashing in to shop tomorrow, Harriet," said Mummy. "So you can come with me and will you make the brandy butter again this year?"

"Yes," I answered quickly, because I adore brandy butter.

"And James, you'll do the tree again, won't you?" asked Mummy.

It didn't feel like Christmas. Broncho had set our minds elsewhere and now I wasn't ready.

Lunch was over now. "Let's put it off," I whispered to Ben. But he shook his head. "You can shop when we get back, we won't be late," he said. "And do stop fussing. You won't be hurt. I'm not asking *you* to ride him."

"It's not that," I answered. "It's just that I don't want anything to go wrong before Christmas."

"It won't. I promise," said Ben with a wide grin. "I'm looking forward to this afternoon. I love challenges."

"Well, I don't," I answered, following him towards the stables, filled with trepidation.

# Four
## "Stop him, for God's sake!"

I tacked up Lorraine. The yard was full of slush, but outside, on the common, the snow was still white and thick, only wet at the edges like melting ice cream.

Ben fetched his bicycle and leaned it against the wall. He tacked up Broncho, while I mounted Lorraine. He tucked the reins under the stirrup irons and attached a headcollar rope to the bit.

"Are you ready?" he asked. I pulled up my girths, Lorraine was anxious to be off. I looked at my watch and it said two o'clock. Ben was putting on the cross-country helmet we share, pressing the fasteners together. He was wearing his rubber riding boots, two jerseys, jeans and an anorak. He handed me the headcollar rope and I thought, this is it, and pushed Lorraine on with my legs; and at the same moment, Lisa came running, crying, "Where are you going? What are you doing?" And Ben said, "Mind your own business. Go away," and mounted his bike. And somewhere, deep within myself, I knew that what we were doing was wrong, that we should have told Mummy, and warned someone that there could be trouble ahead.

"I'm coming," shouted Lisa. "Where's my bike?"

"Punctured," said Ben.

There was no one on the common. Broncho and Lorraine went well together. He was larger and his stride was longer, but she lengthened hers and they kept pace with one another. The trees were emerging from the snow, and the grass, pushing its head through the whiteness, looked green and new. But underneath the snow and the slush, the ground was still hard. Ben was having a tough time on his bike. "Make for the woods," he called. "I'll meet you on the far side, okay?"

"Okay," I shouted.

It was peaceful in the woods and strangely silent because everything was muffled by the snow. The paths looked narrower because of it and were hard to find and the trees were still bowed by the weight they had carried and looked tired, like people who have walked a long way.

Lorraine insisted on trotting and Broncho seemed to be enjoying himself. I could have been happy too if I could have rid myself of the anxiety gnawing at my mind. I tried to sing, but the words died in my throat. I said to myself, "Cheer up, Harriet." But nothing would kill the awful sense of foreboding which hung over me.

I could see beyond the woods now, to the lane where Ben would be waiting. And I could feel the sun trying to push through the clouds and the air growing lighter. I remembered the times I had ridden through the woods before, good and bad times.

"How is he going?" yelled Ben when I reached the lane. "Has he settled yet?"

"If you mean, is he tired? the answer is no," I answered.

"We had better go on, then," he said.

I don't know how many miles we covered. I simply let Lorraine trot on and on, while Ben pedalled behind and the minutes turned into hours. Then, when we had reached the old disused railway track, I drew rein, and said," He's tired now."

The old railway track held memories for me too, good and bad. Ben leaned his bike against a tree, "I'll come back for it later," he said.

"Supposing it's stolen?" I asked.

"It won't be," he said. And suddenly I knew that we were both talking to cover up our fear.

"You don't have to ride him," I said, dismounting.

"What do you mean?" cried Ben.

"He's had a good exercise. We can go back now," I answered.

"Thank you very much," replied Ben. "And I've ridden all this way on my bike – very nice, I must say."

He was checking the fastening on his helmet now, adjusting his anorak, making sure everything was well arranged before he mounted.

"Am I to hold him?" I asked.

"Of course. What do you think?" said Ben.

He was being aggressive because he was scared. I'm scared sometimes; I know what it's like. I'm scared when I'm called to see the headmaster at school; or when I walk home across the common in the dark.

"You can walk with me, lead both horses," said Ben.

Everything seemed very still. There wasn't a soul to be seen, not even a rabbit. I pulled up Broncho's girths. He had got his second wind by this time and was staring into the distance as though searching for something.

"I think we should postpone it," I said. But Ben had his foot in a stirrup now. "Hold on, for God's sake," he said.

The hair was standing up along my spine now as Ben swung his leg across the saddle.

I could feel Broncho growing tense, like a balloon filling up with air and I started to pray, "God, make it all right."

Ben sat down as though he was landing on a row of pins.

He started to talk to Broncho and the air was suddenly full of electricity as before a storm. And then we were moving on and Ben was saying in a relieved voice, "I knew it would be all right." And I said, "Touch wood," but there was no wood to touch.

And we had to go on because we were afraid to turn round. Weeds and grass grew on the track which had been a single-track railway until a few years ago. I could see

34

cows in the distance now, clustered close together, and a tractor on a hill moving slowly and dramatically. Lorraine was reluctant to go on, but Broncho hurried, his eyes rolling backwards, his ears straight upwards with anxiety. I could smell the sweat rising from his body, sending steam into the air. Ben was sitting very still, not daring to move a muscle. He wasn't smiling. It was nearly half-past three now. In half an hour it would be growing dark. I felt full of apprehension.

"We should be turning back," I said.

"In a minute," answered Ben in little more than a whisper. "He's too nervous to turn at the moment."

I thought of Mummy or Mrs Mills putting on the kettle for tea. I thought of Limpet and Puzzle waiting for their hay, and Cassie with her foal Windfall, waiting to come in. The sky was growing darker already. It seemed to promise something – snow or rain? I didn't know which.

"We must go back," I said again.

"Have patience," replied Ben.

"It will soon be dark," I said.

"Try and stop," Ben said after a time. "Try and turn round."

"Whoa, walk," I said as though I was lunging Broncho, "Whoa . . ."

There wasn't much room to turn two horses. Broncho was still very tense, while Lorraine was in a hurry to go home to her warm box and evening feed, and somehow their stirrups caught together. Broncho leapt high into the air. "Hold on," shouted Ben.

Broncho was on the wrong side of Lorraine now, her shoulder between us.

"I'm trying to," I shouted. Then suddenly Broncho was on his hind legs and Lorraine was swinging into him with her quarters. And then one of them knocked me sideways and the next moment I was lying in the snow watching Broncho bucking and then galloping, with my brother still on top, crying "Whoa! Do something, Harriet! Stop him, for God's sake!" And I was scared, more scared than I had ever been before and I saw dreadful tragedy in my mind. Then I was running, shouting, "Stop! Whoa!" And there was nothing anywhere, no help, no house, just the track going on mile after mile, like a miniature race track. And no hope either. The horses were small in the distance already. And I thought, we didn't tell anyone where we were going. They won't know where to look. And I blamed myself for giving in to Ben, for not being strong enough to say "no".

Soon snow and mud hung heavy on my boots, but nothing could be as heavy as my heart. And now it was growing dark and sleet or snow brushed my face, cold and wet.

The track was suddenly hell on earth. And I wished I was someone else altogether – a neat town child living in an apartment, a little girl still at playgroup, anyone but Harriet Pemberton. And then I started to pray,

36

God, make Ben all right. It's all that matters, just Ben. Kill the horses if you must, but make Ben all right.

I could feel tears running down my face, stupid, childish tears. And then the track felt the loneliest place on earth and I saw myself never reaching home, and Mummy sending out search parties and Dad in a rage. And Mrs Mills shouting, "Why didn't they say where they were going?" And Colonel Hunter beginning, "In India we had a golden rule . . ." And Lisa would be crying, and James drinking more and more coffee. At intervals I stumbled on great clods of snow and mud thrown out of the horses' hoofs as they galloped. And then, at last, I saw Ben approaching through the falling sleet, holding an arm, saying, "I couldn't stop them." And, for a minute, the fact that he was alive was all that mattered. Then I saw that one of his arms was hanging in a peculiar way and his face was very white in the gathering darkness. And I said, "Your arm's smashed, isn't it?"

And he said, "Yes, I don't know how it happened."

And I started to cry again.

And Ben, seeing my crying, tried to laugh. "I always was a reckless fool," he said.

"What are we going to do?" I asked next.

"I'll make for the road and help," he said. "Look down, there are lights moving on a road. The lights are cars. It's only two fields away as the crow flies, and I reckon there's only a gate to climb and I can manage that, if you'll just help me through this fence."

"What about me? What am I to do?" I asked.

And then I saw my own dear Lorraine coming back and I knew the answer.

"I'll go on and find Broncho," I said.

"I hoped you'd say that," replied Ben.

# Five
## "Are you all right?"

I helped Ben through the fence. I couldn't
bear to look at his arm.

"How did it happen?" I asked, pointing.

"I don't know. I think my foot caught in
the stirrup and Broncho jumped on my arm.
I'm a bit hazy – sorry," he answered.

"You had the little stirrups. Why didn't
we change them? Why are we such fools?" I
asked.

Ben gave a twisted kind of smile. "Does it
hurt?" I asked.

"Not much. It's kind of numb now." I
watched him walk away into the dusk
towards the cars which looked like shooting
stars on the road below. Then I mounted Lorraine and rode on.

She didn't want to go, but eventually we
were cantering on with sleet in our faces in
the last dwindling light of day. And as I rode
I started to wonder what we would do with
Broncho now. Would he have to be killed?
Was there no more hope? And I knew we had
failed. We had rushed instead of taking our
time. And I knew that with horses the
saying, *more haste, less speed* is true a

hundred times over. And because of that Broncho's last chance was gone.

Lorraine felt tired now, and the mud and the snow were heavy in her hoofs, and the sleet was turning into hail which hit our faces like bullets until we could hardly see anything any more; my feet were freezing in my boots, and my gloves were wet and flabby on my freezing hands.

Then, after a time, I realized that the hail had become snow and was falling like confetti from the night sky. I had been riding in a sort of dream for an hour or more and had reached the old station with the signal box before it. Lorraine's mane was heavy with snow now and my hands were the colour of raw beef. It's time to go back, I thought. I shall never make it if I stay out any longer. And then I heard a whinny and saw Broncho standing beyond the signal box, with his reins broken and his saddle hanging over one side. He looked very tired, and I dismounted and called to him and he stood shaking like a leaf, as though he expected a beating. I waited and he came to me and stood waiting to be taken home, and I knew that this was a victory, though a hollow one. I put his saddle straight with numb fingers and then I remounted and turned Lorraine's head for home. The snow was growing thicker and it wasn't falling like confetti any more but thick and fast in the biggest flakes I had ever seen.

And suddenly I was frightened. It was six

o'clock and we were a long way from home. The snow was balling in the horses' hoofs now, so at times Lorraine felt as though she was on stilts and, because of that, we couldn't hurry. Everything was silent, so that I had the feeling that we were the only things left alive in the whole world.

When we came to the end of the track, I turned the horses' heads for the road below. The snow was very deep now and we slid down a long hill and low branches smothered me with snow. The snow in the horses' hoofs made them clumsy and I started to wonder about Ben. Where was he now? Had he been given a lift home? Was he in hospital having his arm mended? Or had he fainted somewhere and was now dying from exposure? Because I was tired, everything started to seem very bad and I began to cry again. I left everything to Lorraine now and she found her way down a track which led to the road, through snow and branches and over the ruts underneath.

Cars were moving very slowly along the road in single file. They were revving up and skidding and it looked like some crazy game down below and I wondered how we would survive on the road, but I couldn't turn back now because the snow was too deep and we were too tired.

I halted the horses, and we stood and stared and I swear that all our hearts sank when we looked at the traffic. There were men pushing cars and men digging with shovels, and women screaming at no one in particular. There were cars in a ditch and cars across the road and a beautiful new Renault upside down. The horses raised tired heads and looked, and I felt some of the spirit go out of Lorraine. And I said, "We must go on."

It was very slippery on the road. People looked at us as though we were mad and several people shouted unprintable words at us and one jolly man called, "Give us a tow." And Lorraine slipped on to her knees, while Broncho's hind legs slipped under him so that he was sitting on the road. Somehow they struggled into standing positions again and I thought, help must come soon – sanding lorries, snow ploughs, something. I dismounted on to numb feet and pulled snow-wet reins over Lorraine's head and suddenly I didn't know which way to turn for home. I stood and stared at the road and I knew we couldn't travel along it; and I looked back to the track we had come down and it was black as night. And the horses recognized my despair and hung their heads. Then a young man came across the road towards me. He had long hair and spots on his face, and tattered jeans, and he was very thin and there was a gap in his teeth.

He asked, "Are you all right? You're not going to faint, are you?"

And I said, "No, I'm not, thank you. Do I look like it, because actually I'm quite all right, thank you; it's just the road . . ." and

I knew my voice sounded as though I was on the verge of tears.

"Is there anyone you can phone?" he asked. "There's a phone-box just twenty yards on and I can hold your nags if you like."

"I haven't any money," I said.

"Well, I have. I can't move my old bus anyway, so I don't mind waiting," he said. "Walk on the verge and you'll be all right."

He gave me some money and took the reins from me.

When I reached the box there was a man inside shouting at the AA. He was wearing a suit and carrying an umbrella and a small case, and he was very angry. Finally he came out swearing under his breath and said, "Don't be long. I want to telephone the Home Secretary, this is disgraceful. Where are the sanding lorries?"

My fingers were numb and I dropped the receiver twice, but then I was talking to James, saying, "I'm stuck on a road and I can't move, the horses can't stand up. Has Ben come home?"

"Ben's gone to hospital," he said. "Where are you?"

"I don't know."

"Look on the receiver, it says somewhere. Don't be a fool," replied James.

"It says *The Ridgeway*," I answered.

"Okay," replied James. "We'll pick you up."

"I've got two horses," I shouted. But he had rung off. I wondered how they would manage without Ben. He knows how to manage the Land Rover, when to push down the yellow knob, or when to put it in four-wheel drive. Mummy is not mechanical and Dad would still be at work. I found the young man still holding the horses.

"All right?" he asked. "Everything in order?"

"Yes, thank you very much," I said.

Some of the cars had gone but more kept arriving, and then grinding to a halt. Three men were turning the Renault over.

"You look a bit pale. How about some coffee?"

"Yes, please."

His car was old and battered; the sort the police stop to demand an MOT certificate, insurance, licence. One of its bumpers was tied on with string. The coffee was luke-warm and the cup I drank it from had sugar encrusted to the edge, but it didn't matter.

"Have you had an accident?" he asked when I had finished drinking and handed back the cup.

"Not me, my brother."

"Bad?"

"Yes, smashed-up arm." I didn't want to talk about it, because thinking of it made me feel sick.

"He's not up there, is he?" he asked, pointing at the hills.

"No, he's in hospital."

"Do you want another coffee?"

"No thank you."

"I'll stay with you until someone comes."

"I'll be all right," I answered.

A breakdown lorry had appeared and two AA vans and a police car. And the snow wasn't falling any more.

"Who's coming for you?"

"I don't know, just someone," I answered.

"If you could put your horses somewhere, I could take you home," he said.

"I'm all right. You had better go," I said. "You've been marvellous."

He looked at the police car and said, "Okay, if you're sure you're all right."

And I said, "Yes. And thanks a million for saving me."

"Don't mention it," he answered.

And then I saw the bright lights of a Land Rover and trailer, and the horses pricked their ears. I felt hope come back.

I waved to my rescuer and shouted, "I'm all right now. Look!"

And he shouted, "Bye for now."

And then the Land Rover was slithering to a halt and James was yelling at me. "Hurry up. Get the ramp down. There's only me. Why didn't you tell me the police were here?"

"Where's Mummy, then?" I shouted back.

"In hospital with Ben. What do you think?" yelled James, leaping out of the trailer. "And a lot of new guests have arrived and it's utter chaos at home – hell on earth."

We had the ramp down now. James had

forgotten headcollars. "They'll have to travel loose," he said. "Hurry up, will you."

The police were questioning my rescuer now, and a young officer with a moustache was writing in a notebook.

Luckily the horses boxed without any fuss. I threw up the ramp.

"We'll turn at the next crossroads," said James.

He drove too fast. I could feel the trailer rocking behind us. The Land Rover was in four-wheel drive and made a lot of noise.

"Why did you do it?" he shouted.

"Do what?"

"Go all that way without telling anyone where you were going," shouted James.

I didn't answer for a bit; then I said, "Because we didn't want to be stopped."

"Fools! You knew you were wrong, then, and look at the trouble you've caused. I'm breaking the law because of you. And the house is full of demented guests – all because of you."

He turned down a side road and the Land Rover skidded and he pushed down a yellow knob and suddenly the day seemed to have lasted for ever and I started to long for bed, for peace and warmth and a great mug of hot soup.

"I suppose the guests are having my room," I said.

"No, they all crammed together in the attic – five kids and one incapable mother. Mummy had to take them in. She said it was almost Christmas and she couldn't turn them away, because it would be like Mary and Jesus and no room at the Inn.'

"Are they going to be with us for Christmas, then?" I asked.

"Yes, and the food will run out and they've brought two frightful dogs. They were evicted, if you know what that means."

"Of course I do – turned out. But who's paying?" I asked.

"Social services, of course," replied James, nearly hitting a car coming the other way. "You know how Mummy is, she believes every hard luck story she hears. I don't know what Dad will say when he comes home."

"They sound nice," I said through chattering teeth.

We were nearly home now. I could see the common still white with snow, the pond romantic in the moonlight, familiar trees suddenly strangers in their coats of snow.

At that moment I loved home more than ever before. It was all I wanted – the warm kitchen, the smell of supper and my bed waiting for me.

Lisa was toiling in the stable yard.

"At last," she shouted. "Everything's ready. Just put the horses in and go away. I can manage."

James stopped the Land Rover with a jerk.

Inside the horses were soaked with sweat. They fell out on trembling legs and looked round the familiar yard with pleased eyes. Their boxes were ready, thick with straw,

47

with bulging haynets and water buckets full
to the brim.

"Go away," shouted Lisa. "I can manage.
Go in and get warm."

"What about Broncho?" I asked.

"I can manage," shouted Lisa. "I'm not six
years old."

James was unhitching the trailer now. I
was shaking all over with cold and exhaustion and now I could hear dogs yapping and
a strange voice yelling, "Shut up, will you. I
*said* shut up. Do you want a thrashing?" And
somewhere a baby was crying.

Then Mrs Mills opened the door to call, "Is
that you, Harriet? Come in, dear, at once.
You must be half dead . . . !"

And I told my shaking legs to walk and
they walked, while behind me I could hear
Lisa shouting, "Stand up, Broncho, will you.
Get over" – as though she handled him every
day of the week – and James putting the
Land Rover away.

# Six
# Christmas Eve

Our new guest was called Mrs Cutting and she had five children of various ages, and a scruffy dog called Trixie and another larger, smooth-coated one called Spot. Mrs Mills introduced me, but my mind went blank and I could think of nothing to say. Mrs Cutting said, "Pleased to meet you." She was hardly taller than Lisa and her hair was turning grey and her face was a mass of wrinkles. She can't have been more than forty but she looked much older. She kept calling to the dogs, "Sit down, Spot," she shouted, and "Off that chair, Trixie, you're not at home." And when she wasn't shouting at the dogs she was screaming at her children.

I wondered how long Colonel Hunter and Dad would stand her, while Mrs Mills pushed a mug of steaming tea into my hand and my feet started to come back to life.

James had started to decorate the Christmas tree and a heap of new Christmas cards had arrived, including one from a previous guest of ours called Commander Cooley. It came from one of Her Majesty's prisons. I couldn't believe that Christmas had almost arrived – another Christmas. My mind kept returning to Broncho and I thought, they can't shoot him on Christmas Day.

Then Mummy returned, calling, "Where's Harriet? Isn't she back yet?" And I called, "Yes, I'm here. I'm all right."

"They are keeping Ben in overnight," she said, looking me up and down. "Are you all right?"

"Yes."

"However did you get the horses home?" she asked.

"It's a long story," I answered, not wishing to get James into trouble. "How is Ben? Is he unconscious?"

"They are setting his arm now. They had to wait for the consultant to come. It's a bit complicated," replied Mummy. "But he'll be all right. Whatever made you do it, Harriet?"

"Do what?" I asked to gain time.

"Go out so late without telling us where you were going," replied Mummy.

"It's a long story," I said again.

"He'll have to go," Mummy answered.

"Who?"

"Broncho. You can't keep him. He isn't safe. He's bad," replied Mummy. "There must be bad horses, just as there are bad people, and he's one."

"But it was our fault," I said. "We rushed him. We tried to move too quickly. We didn't give him time. It wasn't his fault at all. He's all right. He's super, honestly, Mummy."

"You can't manage him on your own,"

answered Mummy. "And Ben can't help you now, so he must go."

"Not until after Christmas," I answered desperately.

"Why?"

"Because it isn't Christian to kill a horse at Christmas," I said.

"You'll have to telephone Mrs Nuttal," said Mummy, as though I hadn't spoken. "You can ask her to take him away. You needn't ask to be paid anything, just let her take him away and let her vet put him down. Now don't argue, do it . . ."

"I can't," I said. "My lips won't speak the words, my feet won't take me to the telephone. I can't anyway without asking Ben. He's in it too, Mummy. He's broken his arm but he won't want to give in. Please."

"Leave it until the morning, then," replied Mummy after a short silence. "You'll be stronger then."

"I'll wait until Ben is home," I said. "He'll know what to say."

It was late now and no one had had any dinner and Colonel Hunter was sitting in the dining room coughing at intervals to draw attention to himself.

Mummy grilled chops, while Mrs Mills cooked potatoes, and Mrs Cutting said, "I'd rather eat in the kitchen if you don't mind, and the kids can have bread and jam upstairs."

She had brought tins of dog food, a potty, baby clothes and nappies and not much else.

I said, "What are your children called?" And she answered, "Millie, Pete, Jimmy, George and the baby is Samantha, that's a lovely name, isn't it?"

"Super," I said. I had changed now into dry jeans and a polo-necked jumper and I was warm for the first time in hours. And I was beginning to feel more optimistic. The afternoon and evening seemed like a nightmare now. Outside the snow had stopped falling and there was a proud, pale moon riding high in the sky.

"The horses are all right," said Lisa, coming into my room. "And guess what – I've been sitting on Broncho's back."

"You haven't!" I cried.

"I have. Do you want to see? He's as quiet as a lamb."

"No, thank you – just don't tell Mummy, that's all," I said.

"I got on off the partition. He didn't mind at all. He smelt my foot, if you want to know," continued Lisa. "It was dead easy."

"He's tired, dead tired," I said. "He won't be the same tomorrow."

"He's not going to be shot, is he?" asked Lisa.

"Not if I can help it."

"He's so beautiful. We must call him Prince when he's schooled. We can't go on calling him Broncho when he's perfect," said Lisa.

"That's a long way away," I answered.

"But he will be one day, won't he?" asked Lisa, staring at me with worried brown eyes.

"I hope so . . . !"

Dinner seemed to last for ever. Mrs Cutting wouldn't stop talking and Colonel Hunter kept ringing the little bell on the dining room table and wanting things like mustard. And I missed Ben.

Dad came in late and I left Mummy to talk to him. But later he sat on my bed and said, "Harriet, you must try to be more responsible or we'll have to give up keeping horses. You broke the golden rule, didn't you? You didn't tell us where you were going. You must always say – mountaineers have to do it, so do yachtsmen if they've got any sense. It's not fair on the people left behind. If things had worked out differently, we could still be looking for you. Now tell me exactly what happened."

So I told him, beginning at the beginning and ending with telephoning home. But he said, "Go on, how did you get home? You haven't finished, have you?"

And I answered, "I'm not saying unless you promise not to be cross."

"Who with?"

"Any of us."

"All right."

So I told him how James had come and rescued me and he said, "I can't blame him, given his age and the situation. I would have done the same but it mustn't happen again, Harriet, you see that, don't you? Because he isn't covered by insurance and if there had been an accident we could be paying damages for the rest of our lives. And what if he'd been hurt as well – perhaps crippled for life? That would be terrible, wouldn't it?"

"Yes, but I didn't ask him to come," I answered. "And now what about Broncho?"

"Let's leave that until after Christmas. I can't face any more difficulties just now. Just forget him until Boxing Day," said Dad, who isn't horsey so doesn't know that you can't just forget horses. So he kissed me good night and Mummy came in too and said, "Sleep well, Harriet darling, and don't bother to get up early. I've just telephoned the hospital and Ben is all right, so there's nothing to worry about and it's nearly Christmas . . . so don't do anything silly tomorrow, will you, because we don't want Christmas spoilt."

"What about the Cuttings?" I asked.

"They'll be all right. I'm just organizing their stockings, she answered, kissing me good night. And I fell asleep instantly into that heavy dreamless sleep which comes with complete exhaustion.

I overslept the next morning and when I rushed down to the stables, I found Lorraine and Broncho standing at the back of their boxes, looking very tired. They both whinnied a welcome and I looked them over for cuts and scratches but found none. Presently Mike, one of our lodgers, appeared and helped me muck out. He has red hair and freckles and is immensely strong. He isn't clever, but he's kind and likes horses, and though his father is in and out of prison the whole time he's as honest as the day is long. He is nearly sixteen and has a girlfriend called Karen who lives in the village, so we don't see much of him. Soon he'll leave school and work permanently at the nearby farm where he's been helping out for more than a year. But today, at any rate, he decided to help me. "Seeing that Ben isn't 'ere," he said with a grin. "And Christmas is just round the corner. I hear you had a bit of a to-do yesterday one way and another. What happened?"

So I told him as we mucked out, and slowly the sun came out and everything started to drip with melting snow.

Later Mummy took me shopping and I bought her a lipstick and a book of cartoons for Christmas, and Dad a packet of cigars, and Mrs Mills two large handkerchiefs and Mike a penknife. I had already bought my brothers and Lisa books, and Colonel Hunter a calendar with pictures of India on it.

Mummy bought the Cuttings presents as well as things for their stockings and she looked exhausted. When we had finished shopping, we collected Ben from the hospital. He was waiting for us looking very clean and smelling of antiseptic with a large plaster cast on his arm.

"Thank goodness you've come," he cried.

"I've been waiting for ages. Is Broncho all right? He's not dead, is he?"

So I told what had happened for the third time and the sun was still shining and I couldn't believe that tomorrow would be Christmas Day.

"How will we manage now?" asked Ben when I had stopped talking.

"How do you mean?"

"Without me," he answered.

"I shall ride him," I said.

"No, you won't, he's going back," replied Mummy quickly. "He's going back directly Christmas is over."

"It's not over until Boxing Day," I said to give myself more time.

"You'll never ride him," said Ben. "You couldn't stay on the sort of bucks he gave yesterday, nobody could."

"He was scared," I answered. "If he isn't scared, he won't buck."

"He's going back," repeated Mummy.

"We can't always win," added Ben. "And you'll have enough to do looking after the other horses without my help."

"Mike and Lisa are helping," I answered.

"We're back at school in two weeks."

"A lot can happen in two weeks," I replied.

"And you know they'll grow tired of helping after two days, they always do," said Ben.

We were home now and I could see Broncho looking over his box door. Lisa was showing the Cutting children Limpet and Jigsaw, saying, "I'll teach you to ride after Christmas. I promise."

The sky was now a dazzling blue. I gave Lorraine and Broncho oats from my pocket, while Ben watched, saying, "He's beautiful, isn't he? A dream of a horse. It's a pity he's going to end up as dogs' meat."

"He isn't going to," I answered. "Lisa sat on him last night and he didn't do anything . . ."

"What, in the box? She could have been killed!" cried Ben. "You wait until I speak to her. Supposing she had been thrown against one of the walls? I bet she wasn't wearing a hat either."

"Mummy doesn't know," I said. "Don't make it public, Ben. Just tell me what happened to you yesterday."

"I thumbed a lift. I chose a Land Rover so it didn't skid and the bloke drove me straight home. He was a very nice bloke, and he took me right to the front door. He was worried about you, though, but I said you were like a bad penny, you always turned up again," related Ben, smiling. "I knew someone would rescue you, because it's always easy to get help if you're a girl."

"Thank you very much," I said.

It was lunchtime now. I had my lunch in the kitchen with the Cuttings, because I didn't want to do my hair, and Mummy won't let you eat in the dining room unless you're what she calls "respectable". Ben had his lunch there for a change and so did James, because he couldn't bear the Cuttings' chatter. After lunch I made the brandy butter. Then Lisa and I wandered down to the stables and I put the cross-country helmet on and said, "Come on, we'll lunge Broncho for a bit and then I want you to hold him while I get on." And poor Lisa turned pale and said, "What will Mummy say?" and I replied, "This is his last chance. Do you want him shot? He knows us now."

The cross-country helmet was covered with dried slush and so was Broncho.

We tacked him up and then lunged him, first with the stirrups up and then dangling against his sides. Then we filled up sacks of straw and hung them over the saddle and lunged him with them on and we talked to him all the time. He still looked proud and his stride was long and low and tireless but he looked relaxed too and Lisa said again, "He really should be Prince . . ."

And then the moment had come to mount and I tried to keep very calm, because horses are supposed to be able to smell fear. The stirrups were already down and Lisa fed Broncho pony nuts while I mounted, and though he moved slightly as I sat down in the saddle he didn't tremble. He had a marvellous sloping shoulder and his ears seemed miles away and my legs didn't reach as far as the line of his stomach. "Do you want to move yet?" asked Lisa in a small scared voice. And I said, "Not yet," and sat stroking his neck and talking to him. Then I said, "Just three steps and then more pony nuts, please." And we moved on and I saw how small Lisa was to hold a horse of fifteen hands and knew that, if he decided to take off, she would never hang on. But he didn't take off. We walked round the front paddock three times and I could feel him relaxing underneath me. "Let's stop. Supposing someone sees us?" asked Lisa then. And I answered, "They won't. They are far too busy getting ready for Christmas." We walked round once more and then I dismounted very slowly and patted Broncho until my arm ached.

"He won't be shot now, will he?" asked Lisa, relaxing at last.

"I don't think so. I think he's going to be all right," I said, leading him back to the stable.

We untacked him and fetched him a feed.

"Why did he buck Ben off?" Lisa asked.

"Because we rushed him and the stirrups banged together and he was scared," I said. "And Lorraine got in a state too and they started galloping. He probably thought he had a tiger on his back."

We settled the horses for the night and twilight came and I felt full of hope and saw myself riding Broncho through the wintry countryside.

"Don't tell the others. Don't tell them anything. We'll give a display on Boxing Day," I told Lisa. "And won't they be surprised!"

I held on to the gate as I spoke because I believe in "touching wood". And now James was calling "Tea!" and Dad was home, and it was less than twenty-four hours to Christmas Day.

"Listen – carol singers," said Lisa as we walked towards the house. "Next year I'm going to sing carols."

# Seven
## A telephone call

Christmas was fantastic. My stocking was full of useful things like Sellotape, pens, hair shampoo, chocolate and a tie pin with a horse on it. Mrs Cutting rose very early and brought us all tea in bed, while Mrs Mills made coffee and laid the tables for breakfast. Later we all went to church. I was out of practice and lost my way in the service and Mike sang very loudly, while Colonel Hunter knew everyone and enjoyed being social. Then we opened our presents and I had a new riding coat from my parents and lots of super things from everyone else. We had Christmas dinner at lunchtime because of the Cuttings, and after we had digested it Lisa and I slipped outside and I rode Broncho. Lisa led me at first but after ten minutes she unclipped the leading rein and I rode him alone. I only walked and I concentrated on stopping and starting saying "Whoa" when I wanted him to stop and "Walk on" when I wanted him to move off, just as when we lunged him, and he understood. Finally I trotted a few steps and then we decided he had done enough. We tried not to feel too triumphant knowing that "pride comes before a fall", but we couldn't help feeling hopeful.

"We've won!" cried Lisa. "He won't have to be shot now; we've saved him."

"Don't speak too soon," I cried.

"Why was he so crazy?" asked Lisa. "What had happened to him before he came? What made him like he was?"

'I don't know; perhaps one day we'll find out," I answered.

"Won't Mrs Nuttal be surprised?" asked Lisa next. "When will you tell her?"

"Not yet, not until we're sure," I answered.

"Why hasn't she rung up? If she loved him she would have rung up," cried Lisa.

"Perhaps she heard about Ben – news travels fast – and she was afraid our parents would be angry," I answered.

"Poor Ben. He's out of it now, isn't he?" asked Lisa.

"He can still advise," I answered. "But it's been a most peculiar Christmas, hasn't it?" I asked. "Quite different than any other."

"And now it's almost over," cried Lisa. "And Mummy says there's new guests coming; a married couple who like rambling – they are tweedy, she says, and slightly peculiar and called Mr and Mrs Trippet."

The sun shone on Boxing Day. Mike and Lisa helped me with the mucking out and feeding, while the older Cutting children followed us around getting in the way. Lisa and I tacked up Broncho and lunged him, and then I rode him on my own, while Lisa disappeared indoors to fetch our parents. He was rather fresh and ready to shy at anything and Spot ran in and out of the paddock yapping, which didn't help, while the Cutting children sucked sweets throwing the papers in the mud. I wondered how Ben would feel when he saw me riding Broncho. He might be angry or jealous or pleased. He had spent most of Christmas asleep. Mummy said that he was still suffering from shock. But now Lisa was running towards me calling, "They're coming," And Bronco had his ears pricked and was prancing.

"Oh Harriet, I told you not to ride him," called Mummy. "You are naughty!"

"Absolutely disgraceful!" shouted Dad.

"But he's all right," I called. "Look."

I trotted him round the paddock and Dad called, "How did you do it?" And I said, "I don't know; trust, I suppose," and all the time I could feel a sense of triumph running through me. We've done it, I thought, we've succeeded. He won't be shot now.

"It's most extraordinary," continued Dad. "I didn't think you had it in you, Harriet."

Ben was standing behind him now saying nothing and I didn't know what to say either.

"Well done! When are you going to ring up Mrs Nuttal and tell her the good news?" asked Mummy.

"Not until we're certain," I answered. "I want to hack him first."

And still Ben said nothing.

"Don't go alone then and tell us where you are going *this* time," pleaded Mummy.

"You bet I will," I answered.

"He's certainly a beautiful horse," said Dad. "And very valuable, I should say." They were turning to go indoors now. I slid to the ground.

"We'll take him out tomorrow," I told Lisa.

"I can't believe it's true," she said. "That all this is really happening."

"By the way, Mrs Mills is leaving tomorrow, her daughter has turned up in England. She's going to live in a granny flat. We'll miss her, won't we?" asked Mummy.

"I shall," said Lisa, wiping her eyes. "Who will mend my socks when she's gone, or play Memory with me? Does she have to go, Mummy?"

"She wants to be with her grandchildren," replied Mummy. "It's only natural."

"I wish she was unnatural, then," said Lisa.

"Well done, Harriet," said Ben, suddenly smiling. "How did you manage it?"

"I don't know, I think he wants to be good really. He doesn't like being a rogue," I answered.

"I don't think he likes men," suggested Lisa.

"Anyway, he won't have to be shot now," said Ben.

"Does your arm hurt? I'm just sorry it wasn't you riding him just now," I replied. "It seems so unfair, somehow."

64

"No, it doesn't hurt, and perhaps you're better for him," answered Ben. "You seem to suit him, you go together. I like a more solid horse, something which never hots up. I like a horse which will go through anything, face anything. I haven't much patience, have I?"

"I wouldn't know," I answered. "But you're better at staying on than me and braver by far."

The next few days rushed by. I rode Broncho every day while we turned the others out to exercise themselves, except for Lorraine who Lisa rode with me, sitting up very straight and looking like an expert.

Mrs Mills left and Lisa cried and we all missed her; then the Cuttings were found a house to live in by the Council and the Trippets came. Mr Trippet had a small, neat moustache and glasses and Mrs Trippet had dark hair which fell like a curtain on each side of her face. Mummy said that Mr Trippet wrote, and Dad said they were something to do with films, but no one seemed quite sure. Lisa said that they looked like spies and James thought that Mr Trippet was an arsonist and would set fire to the house one night when the moon was high. Ben said that he was certain they smoked pot in their room at night and Colonel Hunter said that Mr Trippet wasn't quite a gentleman.

After a few days they became interested in the horses and were always hanging round the stables asking tiresome questions like,

"Why don't you bed on sawdust?" and, "Are you going to clip the horses out before the spring?" Then Mr Trippet began to talk about Broncho, "He's just the sort of horse that does well in films," he said. "They like that chestnut colour and a pale mane and he carries himself so well. How about it? Would you sell him? I'm sure I could get a couple of thousand for you."

Finally I had to admit he wasn't ours and then, of course, the inevitable questions followed. I had sent a postcard to Mrs Nuttal after Boxing Day saying "*All going well, am riding Hillingdon Prince, hope you will come and see him soon.*" And I had received a postcard back saying, "*Well done! Will telephone,*" Nothing more.

So I said to Mr Trippet, "He belongs to a Mrs Nuttal but she doesn't want to sell." And he said, "Where does she live?" and I had to say, "Middlesex". And I looked at Mr Trippet and I didn't trust him. I didn't know what to do.

I took my anxiety to Dad, but he only said, "Look, Harriet darling, the horse does belong to Mrs Nuttal and if Mr Trippet wants to make an offer for him we can't interfere, can we? And how do you know Mrs Nuttal doesn't want two thousand pounds? Do be reasonable."

"But he's not ready for a change of homes," I answered. "He needs time to settle. He's at a very crucial time in his education."

"Well, I don't suppose Mr Trippet will do

anything – he's just interested, that's all," replied Dad. "He's interested in everything. He wants to buy the Turkish mat in the sitting room and Mummy's china ornaments. He wants to make a quick buck. He's after someone's oak chest as well, I'm told."

"China ornaments and oak chests don't have hearts and minds," I replied, more worried than ever. "Why do we have such peculiar guests?"

"They aren't peculiar, everyone likes making a quick buck," answered Dad. "He's been down to the farm and offered three hundred pounds for an old horse bus they've got there. He's a collector of sorts."

"Of all sorts," I said. "But tell him to keep his grubby hands off Broncho, please."

But now Mr Trippet was always hanging around Broncho, saying, "Can I see him gallop?" and "What's he like over fences?" Questions I refused to answer. And the New Year had come and it seemed time to ring up Mrs Nuttal and ask her over. I started to feel mixed up over Broncho and Ben said, "You're a fool, Harriet. If we are going to take horses to train, we can't be sentimental over them; they'll have to come and go; you can't keep track of all of them."

"But Broncho's special."

"They'll all be special to you," answered Ben.

But I knew it wasn't true. There was an affinity between us, something indescribable, which only a horseman would understand.

To hit Broncho would have been an insult. He wasn't like a normal horse. I never carried a stick on him. We hadn't broken him; we had come to an agreement. And I couldn't bear the thought of anyone riding him without understanding him first.

The Trippets were constantly disappearing, and returning with things which they sorted in their bedroom – one day it was a wooden rocking horse, another day a pewter tankard. James called them "their foraging expeditions" and compared them to hounds foraging for food.

Then one evening near the end of the holidays when we were in the kitchen talking about our guests, Dad said, "You know, some people can't resist a bargain when they see one. It's a compulsive thing; almost a mania. Finally they live for nothing else. I think the Trippets are like that, they are always searching, their room is full of *Exchange and Mart* and local papers with bargain pages. Sometimes I feel I could be the same."

"I heard Mr Trippet talking to a film company yesterday on the telephone," said Lisa. "I didn't hear it all – just the beginning really because I didn't want to eavesdrop."

My heart had given a jump and I felt sick suddenly.

"Did he mention a horse?" I asked.

"Yes," replied Lisa beginning to sniff. "I was afraid to tell you. I kept putting it off. He said he had found a beauty, just right for

68

the part, he said. But aren't you pleased? Don't you want Broncho to be famous?"

"It could be marvellous. You could have your name on telly, you know, trained by . . ." said Ben.

"How much money did he mention?" I asked slowly.

"£2,500."

I used a word we're not allowed to use.

"I heard him say, 'Of course, when you've finished with him, he'll be worth twice that . . .' " continued Lisa.

"In fact, you listened to the whole conversation," said Dad.

"Yes," replied Lisa turning crimson.

But now Mummy was calling, "Telephone. It's for you, Harriet." And I said, "Who on earth?" But going to the telephone I thought I knew. I picked up the receiver with a shaky hand and the voice at the other end said, "Mrs Nuttal here," and I thought, this is it! This is Broncho's Waterloo.

"I thought I should tell you that I've sold Hillingdon Prince," continued Mrs Nuttal. "A film company have bought him. They made a very good offer, so good I couldn't refuse it. Now I know it's all due to you, because you've had some sort of film scout staying with you and you've done wonders with Prince, haven't you? So I want you to have something too. Will £250 do? The film company are sending a box tomorrow. Is that all right, dear?"

I wanted to scream, "No!" Instead I said,

"I don't know whether he'll behave; he's still quite nervous."

"Not to worry, dear. I've explained all that and they've got some expert riders just waiting to train him on. Who shall I make the cheque out to? And be ready for the box at ten o'clock, won't you, dear?" finished Mrs Nuttal. Lisa was breathing down my neck listening to every word. Ben was standing in the kitchen doorway straining his ears.

"Write it to Black Pony Inn," I said.

"Thank you, dear," she said and put down her receiver, and suddenly money didn't matter any more, nothing mattered except that Hillingdon Prince was going and he wasn't ready to go . . .

"Why couldn't Mrs Nuttal simply hire him to them for a hundred pounds a week?" I asked.

"He isn't yours to keep," said Mummy, suddenly beside me. "He never was yours. He'll have a lovely home now."

"You're just being selfish," said James. "Why shouldn't poor old Broncho be famous?"

"He's not Broncho any more. He's Hillingdon Prince now," replied Lisa.

"You'll be able to watch him on telly being a wonder horse," said James. "He'll be immortal."

At that moment the Trippets came into the hall and, looking at us gathered together, Mr Trippet said, "Ah, you've heard about the horse! Are you pleased? Quite a rags to riches story, isn't it?"

And Dad replied. "It's tremendous. How are you? Have you accomplished a lot today?"

And Mr Trippet's small moustache twitched and he said, "Not too badly, thank you, just a few knick-knacks and a copper coal scuttle. Not a fortune by any means but passable, I would say. But Mrs Nuttal's giving *you* something, isn't she?" he added smiling at me. "I said you deserved something . . . after all, you've put a lot of work into the horse, haven't you?"

"So has Ben," I answered. "I don't need money anyway, thank you all the same."

"Oh dear, aren't we high and mighty this evening?" asked Mrs Trippet, nudging her husband while I, unable to bear another minute of the conversation, rushed upstairs to my room.

# Eight
## Goodbye to a horse

I couldn't sleep that night. The moon was high in the sky and every time I looked out of the window I could see Broncho's head staring into the moonlit night over his box door.

I lay in bed imagining him uncontrollable again, bucking and rearing like a wild west rodeo horse. I thought, if only they could have given me a few weeks more to make him safe for anyone to ride. I'm not proud of my riding, I am no better than most people; but I had built up a fragile relationship with Broncho which could easily be broken.

In the end I overslept and was woken by Lisa screaming at my door, "Harriet, wake up! It's half-past nine. The horse box will be here in a moment."

She was still in her pyjamas. I pulled on my clothes and raced to the stables where I found the horses banging on their doors and neighing, and they needed everything – hay, water, feeds, grooming, mucking out. Lisa fed, while I fetched water from the kitchen because the yard tap was frozen. Then I started to groom Broncho, working at a frantic speed, while Lisa fetched travelling bandages for his legs, a tail bandage and a rug.

"Why did you oversleep? I was relying on you to wake me," she said.

"Never rely on anyone but yourself," I answered. "Remember the saying, 'Love many, trust a few, learn to paddle your own canoe'."

"You're cross, aren't you?" she asked.

"No, only a bit frantic." And now the horse-box was turning through the gates and I knew it was goodbye to Broncho, or Hillingdon Prince – whatever you called him – and he was the best horse I had ever ridden.

I turned towards the house and could see the Trippets watching us through a window, no doubt congratulating themselves on the money they had made.

And I hated them.

The horse box was large and smart and two girls jumped out and called, "Are you Harriet Pemberton? We've come to collect Hillingdon Prince" – as though I didn't know.

"I'm just putting on some travelling bandages," I said. "They are ours, so I would like them back, please."

The girls were in their twenties. They wandered round the yard looking at our dirty boxes and the hay Lisa had spilt everywhere and I felt ashamed. They wore head scarves, and tweed jackets and jeans with high heeled boots underneath.

I led Broncho out into the winter sunshine and one of them said, "We've brought a rug."

"He's nervous," I said. "He needs time to get used to people."

"Don't worry, we know all about horses. I'm Janet, by the way," said the tallest.

Broncho didn't like the rug. In the end I sent the girls away and Lisa held him while I put it on.

"He is a handful, isn't he?" said Janet. "Never mind, he'll soon settle down with us. We've got a super trainer, a real smasher."

Broncho wouldn't box, he kept looking back at the stables and then standing on his hind legs and swinging round. Finally I suggested that the others should go away, and I talked to him, telling him that it was like school and he had to go, and that we all had to earn our living in the end. He nuzzled my hair and finally he seemed to say, if you are coming too. So I patted his neck and he followed me up and suddenly I was crying.

The girls rushed from behind and shut the partition doors while I tied him up and then climbed through a little door at the front, and Broncho started to neigh, knowing he had been betrayed.

"Well done!" said Janet in tones of relief. "We'll be off, then, and we won't forget to send the bandages back."

They both smiled at us before they climbed into the cab and started up the engine. Broncho neighed again and I could hear his hoofs pounding on the box door. Lisa said, "He doesn't want to go, poor Broncho." And started to cry.

I could see the Trippets moving away from the window now. The box was through the gate and I said, "We must get on, we've got all the mucking out to do. Where's Mike?"

"He's gone out for the day with his girl-friend. Mummy says he was gone by seven," replied Lisa.

"Charming," I said.

We turned out Lorraine, Cassie and Windfall, and Solitaire. The ponies Limpet and Jigsaw slept out all the year round. I couldn't bear to look at Broncho's empty loose box. Presently Ben appeared and said, "I wish I could help. Let me do some forking anyway."

"He's gone," I said.

"Yes, I saw," answered Ben. "And for goodness sake stop crying. You've still got Lorraine, so what's the matter?"

"I didn't want him to go like that. I wanted him to go somewhere near. It was as though he was being taken away to prison. He didn't want to go . . ." I cried.

"He'll have everything," replied Ben. "Food, shelter, experts to sort out his problems – he's so lucky, can't you see?"

But I couldn't. I could only see him leaving us, betrayed by me whom he had trusted and it was almost more than I could bear.

"And think of the money we're getting," continued Ben. "We can halve it. I've asked Mummy and she says it's ours; she and Dad don't want any part of it because we've earned it, me with my broken arm and you with your courageous perseverance."

"I don't think I want it. You can have it all," I answered. "I feel as though I've sold a friend. I can't explain it."

"You'll feel better tomorrow," replied Ben after a short silence. "No one but a nutcase can refuse a hundred and twenty five pounds fairly earned."

Later we went indoors and ate bread and cheese because it was too late for breakfast and too early for lunch and Mummy looked at my tear-stained face and said, "You are a fool, Harriet. You'll never make a horse dealer. You make a fantastic success of something and then you cry. You're completely crazy."

"You'll be famous now as a horse-breaker and trainer," said Lisa.

"It's for the best, anyway. You start school tomorrow and you could never have coped with all the mucking out; you know you couldn't. And when would you have found time for exercising Broncho?" asked Mummy.

"I had worked it all out," I answered. "I was going to get up at six and muck out by electric light and then lunge Broncho before going to school and ride him when I got home. I was going to buy a stirrup light and a fluorescent jacket so I could ride him in the dark."

"It sounds highly dangerous to me," said James, coming into the kitchen. "Has anyone seen my football socks?"

"Not again?" replied Mummy. "You can't

lose your football socks twice in less than a week."

"James can," said Ben.

I could see the Trippets driving away in their Dormobile, no doubt looking for more bargains, their faces eager with anticipation, like dogs looking forward to a walk.

"He's wearing plus-fours," said Ben, following my glance "and smoking a curly pipe, *you* know the sort."

"Colonel Hunter has asked to have breakfast in his room. He can't stand them either. Can't we get rid of them, Mum?" asked James.

"They've paid in advance and they aren't any trouble," replied Mummy. "They're out to lunch today and they won't have anything taken off the bill."

"I wonder when Broncho will arrive," I said. "I wish we knew exactly where he's going. Why didn't I ask? I never ask the right questions."

"Do go and get ready for school," replied Mummy. "I can't bear you all in the kitchen."

I went upstairs and collected my things for school – my overall for science, my blouse and blazer and boring pleated skirt.

Outside, the ground was rock hard again; the mud frozen into shapes as hard as metal; the bare trees decorated with frost-like white icing sugar. On the common, boys were sliding on the pond. So, slowly the day passed. Lisa spent the afternoon playing Memory with Twinkle our cat, though how a cat plays

Memory I've never understood. She was missing Mrs Mills who had been an ever-willing card player. Ben read *Horse and Hound* from cover to cover. James made countless cups of coffee and searched for books he had lost since last term. Mummy filleted fish for supper. I wandered about trying to think about school but thinking of Broncho instead. Lisa and I mucked out in the evening together. Mike was still away and there was a cold wind now which scurried round the yard blowing straw off the wheelbarrow and hay out of our arms. Ben hung about talking about what he was going to buy with his earnings and slowly the day turned into dusk and then into night.

We put our things ready for school before we went to bed and Mummy gave us our lunch money, and Dad gave us a lecture on working hard. The Trippets returned in time for dinner, smelling of whisky, and Ben said that their Dormobile had a heap of valuable glass in it, so obviously they had had a good day. "We'll stay another day or two if that's all right with you," Mr Trippet told Mummy, his moustache twitching. "We've had a most marvellous stay and you've made us most comfortable. We will certainly recommend you to our friends."

I dreamed that night that I was hunting on Broncho. We jumped fence after fence until suddenly we were alone in front of hounds in a moonlit countryside. We seemed to be painted with silver and Broncho's ears were made of glass and then the moon started to come towards us, enormous and terrifying and whichever way we galloped, and we couldn't escape because it was larger than the world. I wakened crying, "Stop, please stop," and heard the post van come into the drive and Mr Trippet opening his window to call something to the postman.

Later, Lisa and I rushed round the horses at top speed, helped by Mike who is very strong but a bit slow on the uptake.

There wasn't time for a proper breakfast. I ran for the school bus clutching a piece of toast and marmalade in my hand.

"It's going to snow some more," said Ben, looking at the sky.

"And then we can toboggan," cried Lisa. "And make a snowman and throw snowballs at each other. How lovely."

School passed slowly. I couldn't concentrate and I didn't seem to have a single friend when breaktime came, which was hardly surprising since I had ignored them the whole holidays. Ben wandered about with his arm in plaster telling everyone of his disaster.

"But all's well that ends well, because Harriet conquered the brute and now he's going on telly," he said. And I wondered why he always talked differently at school, because he would never have used the word "brute" to describe a horse at home.

The playing fields were too frozen for games so we spent the afternoon in the gym and then at last it was time to go home.

Ben and I never talk to one another on the bus. He sits with his cronies and I sit in the front usually on my own.

The bus wanders all over the place before it finally drops us on the common. Lisa is still at Primary so she reaches home before us. Today she met us in the yard shouting, "Harriet, Mrs Nuttal's rung. I don't know what about. You're to ring her back."

"It's probably about the money," said Ben.

"She sounded in a stew," said Lisa.

But now I was running to the house, my heart pounding against my ribs, thinking, "Broncho, something's happened to Broncho."

"She's rung twice," said Mummy as I rushed into the kitchen.

"What can she want?" I yelled. "Where's her number? I don't know what it is."

"I've written it down. Look on the front of the directory. It's in red chalk," said Lisa.

"And calm down," said Ben. "It can't be that important."

"Why wouldn't she leave a message?" I asked, dialling.

"I don't know," replied Lisa. "She didn't say."

Then I could hear her voice at the other end and I said, "Harriet Pemberton here, you rang," and I could feel my heart pounding inside me.

"Yes, I did. I have some bad news – Broncho's gone."

"Gone!" I cried. "Do you mean dead, or stolen? What do you mean?"

"He's escaped. They put side reins on him this morning and he seemed to go mad. He got away with a lunge rein trailing behind him. He jumped a six-foot boundary fence, and he hasn't been seen since."

"With the side reins still on?" I said after a moment, seeing it all in my mind's eye.

"I suppose so. They've told the police, of course. They say he went mad," continued Mrs Nuttal.

"I suppose he'll collide with a lorry," I said.

"He hasn't so far. He's simply disappeared," replied Mrs Nuttal.

"Ask where he was," hissed Lisa.

"Where was he?" I said.

"In the Midlands, near Coventry, I believe."

"But that's miles away," I answered.

"There's nothing we can do. I don't know why I rang you really. I just had to tell someone. I'm so upset," said Mrs Nuttal.

"If only we could search," I answered. "I feel so helpless. And how can he rest with side reins on?"

I looked at my hand and saw that it was shaking. Lisa was crying and Ben was looking out of the window as though the answer to everything lay somewhere in the garden. And I could hear the old clock ticking in the hall and it seemed to be Broncho's heart ticking its strength away. And I didn't know what to say. Suddenly I was lost for words.

So I said, "I'm sorry. Goodbye," and put down the receiver and thought of Broncho somewhere with side reins running from his bit to a roller and a lunge rein trailing behind him and I thought the sight of him must be the saddest sight in all the world. I imagined him rolling in desperation trying to detach the reins and I prayed that they weren't too tight and I thought, I was right, he shouldn't have gone, not for all the money in the world – he wasn't ready.

Then Mummy was beside me saying, "Don't pine, darling, he'll turn up somewhere. He can't get far like that, can he?"

And I said, "He's jumped a six-foot fence." I didn't want any tea. I went outside and fed our horses and Broncho's empty box reproached me. I looked at it for a bit and then bedded it down, and now it looked like a bedroom waiting for someone's home-coming and I thought perhaps the police will find him and bring him home to die. But I knew they wouldn't because he had never belonged to us and he didn't belong to Mrs Nuttal any more either, he belonged to the film company. If he's hurt they'll shoot him, I thought, and he'll be just a £2,500 loss on a balance sheet, nothing more.

Cassie looked over her box into the twilight whinnying and I thought, she's missing him too. But Lorraine was quiet and dreamy and Solitaire his usual self. Lisa wandered about the yard without speaking and Ben filled water buckets carrying them with his good arm and none of us felt like talking. Finally Lisa said, "Poor, poor Broncho. Do you think we'll ever hear what happens to him? They don't have to tell us, do they? I mean, he belongs to them."

And I said, "That's right," and suddenly it was the worst thing of all.

# Nine
## "Funny joke?"

A cheque for £250 arrived the next day from Mrs Nuttal. I handed it to Mummy. "I don't want it," I said. "It's like blood money."

I couldn't concentrate at school. Maths seemed to last forever and I broke a test tube in science. I missed lunch altogether and my eyes strayed to the window all through the cookery class. But, at last, school was over and we were in the bus once more trundling around the villages, taking hours to get home. Lisa was waiting for us in the yard again when we eventually arrived.

"No news," she shouted, "no telephone calls, nothing!"

There was a cold wind and flurries of sleet and a sky colder than the coldest sea.

"It's going to snow again," said Ben, turning up his coat collar and immediately I saw Broncho dying in a snow drift, his proud head slowly sinking to rest in a white grave, his hoofs protruding, slowly to be covered too by falling snow.

The kitchen was warm and welcoming. "We've got some new guests coming next week," said Mummy. "Isn't that lovely?

They're quite young, with a baby, and they want us to babysit for them."

"Super," said Ben without much enthusiasm.

"Any news? Any news at all?" I asked.

"You mean about Broncho?" replied Mummy. "You must be reasonable, Harriet darling. We can't expect news because he isn't ours, so please stop hoping for it, and forget the horse. He isn't our responsibility any more."

"I can't," I answered. "It was so wonderful saving him from the knackers and now this. I can't bear it."

"Oh Harriet," cried Mummy. "Do be sensible; he's only an animal after all."

I didn't mention him again but all the time my heart was aching for news and I kept imagining hoofs coming down the road but when I looked there was nothing. I'm going mad, I thought. Soon I shall start talking to myself.

I dreamed he was swimming in the sea. I kept putting out my hand to touch him but he sank every time before I could stroke his flaxen mane. I went to get help but when I came back in a boat he was gone altogether.

I was wakened by Lisa shaking me, "It's time to get up," she cried. "You've overslept again."

I felt ill all day and snow started to fall again. At twelve o'clock the headmaster, fearing drifts, shut the school and the buses arrived. People threw snowballs at the staff, but Ben couldn't join in because of his broken arm and I felt too ill, so we sat in the bus and talked.

"He can't have disappeared," said Ben. "Horses don't just disappear."

"Couldn't we ring up the film company and ask after him?" I suggested.

"Let's try Mrs Nuttal first," replied Ben.

"He doesn't belong to her either," I answered.

"But he did," said Ben as if it made a difference.

The journey home took even longer than usual. Lisa was waiting for us. "The Trippets are leaving," she said. "Isn't it super?"

"Any news?" I asked.

"No nothing . . ."

We'll forget him in the end, I thought. He'll be nothing but a memory in a few years' time. But I didn't want to. I wanted to know whether he was alive or dead.

The Trippets were loading up their Dormobile in front of the house.

"Any news of the horse?" asked Ben.

"How should I know?" snapped Mr Trippet. "He's not my responsibility."

They looked as though they had had a bad day; his moustache wasn't twitching any more and she looked defeated.

"Good riddance to bad rubbish," muttered Lisa.

I telephoned Jean Nuttal. "Any news?" I asked.

"No, nothing. I don't expect any," she replied.

"Won't they let you know if they find him?" I asked.

"They don't have to." She sounded despondent. I hung up.

"Any news?" asked Lisa.

I shook my head. "There may never be any news as far as we're concerned," I replied. "You see, it's none of our business."

"You mean we may never know whether he's alive or dead?" asked Lisa.

"That's right," I answered. Tears were pricking behind my eyes because now there seemed no hope of anything – news good or bad.

The Trippets were settling their account in the hall. The young married couple had arrived with their baby, so I showed them their room. They admired everything – the staircase, the pictures, the view. Their baby was sweet and called Emma.

"We've just made it and now we're going to be snowed in," said the wife and then, "By the way, call me Janet and my husband's Steve. I'm so looking forward to being here . . ."

"I'm Harriet," I said, holding out my hand.

"I hope there's a big log fire downstairs," said Janet who had long, dark hair and a marvellous *retroussé* nose.

"It's just been lit," I answered. "And you must come and meet Colonel Hunter, he's our longest staying guest. He talks about

India all the time and now if you'll excuse me, I'll go and do the horses."

Lisa helped me feed the horses; it was a long job because everything was weighted with snow. Gates were heavier than usual; buckets were lined with it and our backs became coated with it. But at last everything was done. It was six o'clock now and the snow was stopping and the sky suddenly full of stars.

Janet was breast-feeding her baby in the kitchen when we went indoors again which made Lisa feel shy, for neither of us had ever seen a baby being fed before. Mummy was making soup, Mike was tobogganing with his girlfriend and Ben was talking to Steve about motor bikes.

"For goodness sake dry your hair, Harriet," Mummy said. "It's dripping on everything."

"No news, no telephone calls?" I asked.

"No, and stop asking, there's no point," replied Mummy and started to tell Janet about Broncho.

And then James appeared, his hair on end, a mug of tea in his hand.

"Broncho's alive," he said.

"What do you mean?" I asked. "How do you know? You're just pretending, aren't you?"

"It was on the news," he said.

"Ha, ha," I cried, "funny joke."

"He was really," said James. "He was seen trotting through Banbury. They showed him on telly and he hadn't any reins on or anything much. Honest . . ."

I felt sick with hope. "You're not being funny, are you?" I asked.

"He's heading this way," said James.

"Did they say so?"

"No. It wasn't our usual local news. I was fiddling about and it wasn't very clear but it looked like him."

"Was he covered with snow?" asked Lisa.

"Yes, and the traffic was held up and then he vanished across fields. I'll get a map."

He returned with Ben. "He's travelled miles already," he said. "Look how far Banbury is from Coventry."

"He could yet be killed," said Ben.

"But he's coming this way," I cried. "And he may be all right. Oh, I'm so happy. We know he isn't dead yet anyway. There's still hope."

"He's still over a hundred miles away," said James.

"About three days," said Ben.

"I'll ring up Jean Nuttal. I must. She'll be so pleased," I said running to the telephone. She answered at once. "He's on his way back," I cried. "He's been on telly. He went through Banbury."

"Is that you, Harriet dear?" she said.

"Yes, it's about Broncho."

"But are you sure it's him? Did they say so, dear?" she asked.

"No, but it must be," I answered.

"I don't think so. I don't think he could have got from Coventry to Banbury in that time, dear. It's a long way and then there's the traffic. Don't be too hopeful, dear."

I could feel a battle going on inside me between hope and despair.

Hope won. "It must be," I said and hung up.

"Well?" asked Ben.

"Crushing. Disbelieving," I said. "But I don't care."

"Was it really Broncho? Are you absolutely sure?" I asked James later. "Could you have made a mistake?"

"I've told you it looked like him but the reception was bad because it wasn't in our area," he replied.

We listened to the news on radio all that evening and Lisa stayed glued to the television set until Mummy chased her to bed. But no one mentioned a runaway horse again. I listened for the telephone to ring. I was certain that news would come from somewhere somehow, but it didn't. We were all on edge and there was nothing we could do about it and that was the worst thing of all.

In the morning there was another foot of snow and none of the school buses were running. The snow came to the tops of our boots now and the whole countryside seemed suddenly silent and remote. The post arrived two hours late and the papers didn't arrive at all. And I could only think of Broncho. Was he struggling through drifts to reach us? Or was he dying somewhere of hunger and exposure?

I no longer noticed what I ate. I did everything automatically; and then wondered whether I had done it at all.

Janet seemed to be forever in the kitchen washing nappies or bathing Emma. Dad was at home complaining about dirty fingermarks on the walls and the state of our bedrooms. The house was thatched with snow, the windows edged with it. We cut the horses' oats to nil and later James, Steve and Janet disappeared with toboggans, while Mummy and I watched over Emma.

"You must be tougher, Harriet," said Mummy. "You can't go into the horse business if you're going to become so attached to a single horse. It just won't work. Can't you see?"

"Yes, of course I can," I answered. "But Broncho is special."

"But won't they all be?" asked Mummy.

"No."

I peeled the potatoes for lunch and swept the stairs. But I didn't really see the potatoes and I missed most of the dust on the stairs, because I could see nothing but Broncho – Broncho jumping fences, Broncho trotting on and on. The snow balling in his hoofs, Broncho being caught and taken back to the film company, Broncho dying. I thought I was going mad. And I kept hearing hoofbeats which weren't there. And imagining distant neighing, and the telephone ringing.

Ben said, "You look as though you're in a trance," and waved a hand in front of my eyes to see whether I would blink. When James returned he made coffee for us all which made Mummy read the riot act.

"Coffee is now a luxury," she stormed. "You can no longer drink it like water James, or we will all be ruined."

"Just once in a while," he pleaded.

"No, not even once in a while," stormed Mummy.

"But this is an emergency," he replied.

"No, it isn't. Coffee can now be drunk only after dinner," she said. "And out of small cups, not out of large mugs."

"I'll die," wailed James. "It's my only pleasure in life."

"My arm is itching under the plaster. Anyone got a knitting needle?" asked Ben.

"Can't we ring the police?" I asked.

"But he isn't ours," replied Mummy. "And there's a knitting needle upstairs on the passage window ledge, Ben. Forget him, Harriet. That's my advice."

"Oh, not that again," cried Dad coming into the kitchen. "If anyone mentions that wretched horse again, I'll go barmy."

"Go barmy, then," said Lisa and was sent to her room for being rude.

And the snow continued falling, "snow on snow" as they say in a famous Christmas carol. Lunch was eaten and eventually teatime came. Lisa and I spent the afternoon cleaning tack, while Ben stood about doing what he could with one arm, but mostly getting in the way.

92

Dinner lasted a long time, because Dad opened some wine and we all talked our heads off, because the Trippets had left and our new guests were great fun and always laughing. Colonel Hunter became very merry and chatted up Janet and Dad liked Steve. At ten o'clock I went to bed and, looking at the snow outside, I thought there's really no hope now, no hope at all. He must be dead by now.

I wakened early and listened to the news. A whole family had died in snow drifts and more snow was forecast. There was fighting in Africa and the Conservatives had won a by-election and the dustmen had come out on strike. There was no mention of a horse trotting down a high street or appearing like a ghost on a motorway.

I found Mummy downstairs already laying the breakfast.

"Can't we start looking?" I asked. "The Land Rover would be all right in drifts."

"Looking? Oh Harriet, you're not still worrying about that horse, are you? But darling, we're cut off, look outside. And the deep freeze will soon be empty; I really can't worry about a naughty horse at this period in time."

The snow was six inches over our boots now. We had to dig a path to the stables. In fact we had to dig out the whole yard. Luckily Dad and Steve came to our rescue.

Instead of helping, Lisa made a snowman and Mike threw snowballs at her. I shouted, "Come and help." And then I heard a voice calling me and I went to the yard gate and saw our nearest farmer, Mr Rawlings, sitting on his tractor coated with snow.

"I thought I ought to tell you there's a horse back yonder trying to get up the lane. He's covered with snow and very weak. Is he one of yours?" he asked.

I started to say, "Yes, it's Broncho," and then I was shouting, "He's coming home. Lisa, Ben, he's in the lane . . ."

"I don't know how you'll get him up here," said Mr Rawlings doubtfully. "The snow is three foot deep and he's very weak."

And I thought, he's come home to die. And I said, "Thank you, Mr Rawlings. Thank you very much," but it was only half of me talking because the other half was already making plans, crying, "We'll need ropes. Hurry."

# Ten
## Snow drifts

Mr Rawlings didn't go away. He said, "You may need the tractor. I'll stay." Dad tried to start the Land Rover but it would only groan.

Lisa cried, "I knew he would come home. I never gave up hope."

Ben said, "We'll need the toboggans, we can lay him across them and drag him behind the tractor."

"Get all the spades and shovels together," ordered Dad.

"Could we get a snow plough from anywhere?" asked Steve.

"Let's see how he is first," answered Dad.

"I'll meet you there," said Mr Rawlings, starting up his tractor.

I filled a bucket with oats. Lisa fetched a headcollar. We loaded everything on to the two toboggans and set off. The snow came over our knees on the common. We tried to make a path but it was hard, cold work. Lisa started to cry after a time and had to be sent home. Then we saw that Mr Rawlings was making some sort of path with an ordinary plough and Dad said, "Thank God for Mr Rawlings."

I wanted to run, to throw my arms round

Broncho's neck. But running was out of the question because in places the snow was waist-high now.

"Nobody else would do this for a mere horse," said Dad. "Talk about mad dogs and Englishmen."

"We're never ready for anything in this country, are we?" asked Steve.

"You're dead right," agreed Ben.

"I shall hate snow for ever after this," I said.

"It's like the sea; it's all right until you start drowning," laughed Steve.

Dad and Steve went first because they were the tallest but we didn't seem to be making much progress and there was no one to be seen besides ourselves and Mr Rawlings, not even a dog.

"Why haven't we got snowshoes?" asked Ben who was hardly moving with his broken arm.

"Don't ask a silly question," snapped Dad.

We could see the woods now and the lane which led to them, usually a mere five minutes walk away. Mr Rawlings was in the snow trying to unclog the wheels of his tractor. I could see Lisa, a tiny figure, turning into the stable yard, and now Mike was going back too, muttering, "I'll never make it and I'm not going to risk my life for a horse."

And I was soaked through and my legs were aching from struggling and my feet were numb and I thought, so near and yet so far. God give us strength, please God, he's come so far, he can't die on the last lap. And Mr Rawlings was waving now, calling, "The tractor's broken down. I'll have to go home."

"But how?" yelled Dad.

"I don't know," shouted Mr Rawlings.

And then Dad turned on me and yelled, "It's all your fault, Harriet. It's because of you and your stupid worthless horse. We're all going to die of exposure because of you."

I felt too small and frightened to say anything.

"You're wrong, Mr Pemberton," said Steve. "We came of our own free will. Don't blame your daughter."

The snow was falling faster and faster now and we weren't even halfway to the lane.

"He'll have to die," said Dad at last. "We'll have to go back."

"What about Mr Rawlings?" asked Ben.

"We'll send the police to rescue him. They'll send a snow plough. And don't cry Harriet. We've done our best; we've risked our lives for your damned horse."

"He's come so far," I said.

"That's life," replied Dad.

"You can't reproach yourself with anything," said Steve.

"He was doomed from the beginning. We gave him a few more weeks of life," said Ben.

Dad cupped his hands round his mouth and shouted, "We'll send help to you, Mr Rawlings, not to worry."

Snow blew into our faces and blinded us. "There's going to be a blizzard," said Steve.

"He's probably dead by now, anyway," said Ben. "Frozen stiff; it's a peaceful death, Harriet, you just grow sleepy."

"But he's come so far," I said again. "Couldn't we get the Land Rover started?"

"And drive in this? You must be dotty," replied Dad. "It would be over the wheels . . ."

Our earlier footprints had already vanished. The snow stung our eyes and then Steve cried, "Look, look over there. There's a snow plough; it's clearing the road." And suddenly we were all shouting, "Help, we need you. Help!"

And Mr Rawlings was waving and pointing too. "They won't hear," said Ben. "The snow is muffling our voices."

"They'll hear me," said Steve, holding his breath and then yelling. "Come over here."

"Make for the road, they're clearing it," said Dad.

The two men on the snow plough were wearing goggles. We reached the road following the path we had made, and waved like people on a desert island waiting for a ship to rescue them.

I said, "Will they help with Broncho?"

And Dad replied, "Forget that horse for five minutes, will you?" We were all shivering and my teeth were chattering too, so I seemed to be shaking all over.

"Here it comes," said Steve, whose brown hair was coated with snow.

The men on the snow plough turned down

the engine. "Do you want to die out here?" they shouted. "Why don't you stay at home? Don't you listen to your radio?"

"There is a horse over there," I yelled. "And he's dying. We were trying to rescue him. Is that a crime?"

"What's he doing there?"

"He's come from Coventry," I answered.

"If you can just clear the road, we can manage the rest. We've got a trailer. Could you clear the piece to our yard gate, please? It's just there," said Dad, pointing.

"Then we can get home," added Steve.

They started the engine and we followed the path they made.

Lisa was waiting in different clothes by the gate.

"Have you seen him?" she asked.

"No, but they're clearing the road. The snow plough is here."

"We've got to start the Land Rover," cried Ben, running.

Mummy and Janet and Lisa had dug out the yard for the second time. Steve threw up the bonnet of the Land Rover. "I expect it's the distributor," he said.

"He could be dying now," I said.

"Shut up," replied Ben.

James brought tea. "I'll dig out the trailer," he said. Lisa fetched me dry clothes because I couldn't stop shivering.

"I can hear Emma yelling, I'd better go," said Janet.

Steve had the Land Rover going now. Dad

backed it out. We hitched up the trailer. "Bring the spades," said Dad. "We'll have to dig him out."

"If he's still alive," said Ben.

We threw the spades into the trailer. Another minute and we were driving away along the road which leads round the common to the woods.

"Feeling better?" asked Steve, smiling.

"Yes, but still afraid," I said.

The snow plough was waiting by the lane. "We'll go ahead," shouted the men. "We shouldn't but we will."

Mr Rawlings was there too. "I can always pull him out with the old tractor," he said.

It all seemed a little unreal. I suppose it was the snow. I had never seen so much snow before.

I didn't want to look when we reached the lane. The snow plough had cleared a path and I could see Broncho lying on his side. "He's breathing," said Ben.

"He's alive," screamed Lisa.

"Don't frighten him," said Mr Rawlings. "Keep your voices down."

Dad started to dig his legs out of the snow. I knelt down beside him. He looked exhausted; he smelt my coat and I said, "It's all right, Broncho, you're home." And then, "Give me the oats, Lisa." But he wouldn't eat.

"Careful, don't chop his legs, Dad," said Ben.

"We can get him up now," said James.

"Don't rush him, let him take his time," replied Mr Rawlings, bending down to massage Broncho's legs.

I started to scrape the snow off his sides.

"Poor, poor Broncho," said Lisa.

We pulled his forelegs out and I saw that he had lost a shoe. He was shivering uncontrollably now. I put his headcollar on.

"Gently does it," said Mr Rawlings. "Someone help me with his quarters. Steady now."

I pulled on the headcollar rope but Broncho wouldn't move.

"Give him time," said Mr Rawlings, rubbing his legs again.

"Perhaps he's been blinded by the snow," cried Lisa. "Test his eyes."

"Don't be silly," said Ben.

"Why doesn't he get up, then?"

"Because he's exhausted," said Steve.

"If we don't hurry, the road will be under snow again," said Ben.

"The snow plough is still here," replied Dad, glancing over his shoulder.

"Come on, Broncho, make the effort," I said, my face against his. "You're nearly home and you're never going away again. You're home for good now." And then slowly he began to move, to tense his stiff muscles, to stretch a little.

"Leave him alone," said Mr Rawlings. "Let him do it in his own way." And now Broncho looked at me and nickered and then very slowly he lurched into a sitting position and the next moment he was up, a thin exhausted horse but still alive.

"Take it slowly," beseeched Mr Rawlings. "Let him look about him."

The men on the snow plough were drinking from a Thermos flask. They shouted, "Well done, mate. He's still alive, then?" And Dad shouted, "Yes, mostly thanks to you, because a little longer and he would have been dead for certain."

And they said, "We'll be going then."

Lisa ran ahead to put down the ramp of the trailer and we loaded him slowly and carefully, inch by inch.

And the snow was still falling. Steve cleaned it off the windscreen and then at last we were moving slowly, gently towards home. But first we called our thanks to Mr Rawlings who called back, "It was nothing. I'm glad he's saved. I was afraid he would be dead."

And Dad said, "What a wonderful man." And I said, "We'll never be able to thank him enough, will we?" But no one answered.

Mummy and Janet were waiting for us. "We've arranged his box and made him a mash," said Mummy. "Everything's ready." They were wet to the skin and covered with hay.

"What about lunch?" asked Dad.

"Colonel Hunter's watching the potatoes," said Mummy. Broncho raised his head and gave a great sigh when he saw his box waiting for him and Lisa and I dried him while the others put the Land Rover and trailer away. He drank a little and after a time he ate his mash, so we knew now that he would live.

"It's a miracle, isn't it?" asked Lisa as we put a jute night rug on him with a blanket underneath.

"I shall have to ring Jean Nuttal and tell her," I said. "I must put her out of her agony."

"Not yet, not until after lunch," pleaded Lisa.

"Why?" I asked.

"I don't know. I'm just afraid," she said.

# Eleven
## "He's half dead"

I was afraid too when I dialled Mrs Nuttal's number.

"It's Harriet Pemberton here. Broncho's home," I said.

She gave a gasp. "Are you sure?" she asked.

"He's in the stable," I replied. "He's eating a mash. He is exhausted."

"But how?"

"Under his own steam."

"I can't believe it. I'll have to let the film company know, of course," she said.

"Will they want him back?"

"I expect so."

"Tell her they can't have him," shrieked Lisa down my ear, nearly piercing the ear drum.

"He's not well enough to travel. He's really quite ill. He'll need a vet's certificate. He's half dead. Anyway, we're snowed up. It's impossible to get in and out. The snow plough cleared the road this morning but it's blocked again already," I cried desperately.

"They can't take him away now," cried Lisa.

"I'll tell them what you say. But they have

paid for him and I've cashed the cheque. And you've had your money too, haven't you?"

"Yes, but I haven't cashed the cheque yet," I answered.

"Well, I should," she said. "I'll be in touch. Thank you for ringing, dear. It really is amazing, isn't it? What about the bridle and roller?"

"All gone," I said.

"I'll tell them, dear. Goodbye." She hung up.

"So?" demanded Lisa, hands on hips.

"The film company still own him," I cried, tears blinding my eyes, "And we can't even offer to buy him back, because we haven't two thousand pounds."

"We can hide him, then," said Lisa. "Every time they come, we can pretend he's disappeared. Or we can make him unrideable again."

"Legally he's theirs," I answered.

"Who cares about that? He loves us. We can't let them drag him away again."

"They can't do anything while we're snowed up," said Ben, who had been listening in on the extension upstairs.

"He may be ill," I said. "I'm going to look at him, anyway."

The snow had stopped falling. A robin perched on a gate looking like a bird on a Christmas card, reminding me that it was only a few weeks since Christmas, though it seemed like years. Broncho was lying down. He looked very tired and his sides seemed to be going in and out too fast for normal. "He's probably getting bronchitis," I said.

"He isn't coughing," replied Ben. "If you have bronchitis you cough."

"It's something else, then. We'll have to have Roy." Then I looked at Jigsaw who had been brought in because of the snow and he looked peculiar too. He didn't want to move and, when he did, his quarters didn't move properly. And suddenly Ben and I were both looking at Lisa who turned scarlet. "You've been giving him oats, haven't you?" cried Ben.

"He kept asking, whinnying and nudging me. He was so sweet," replied Lisa.

"So now he has Monday morning disease, better known as azoturia," cried Ben. "Too much protein, in fact, for no exercise. Oh, Lisa!"

And Lisa buried her head in her hands, and screamed, "I didn't mean to. I didn't know."

"Well, you know now and why do you think we cut their oats to nil? Didn't you notice?" said Ben.

"No one told me," cried Lisa.

"We'll have to have Roy now," said Ben. "If he can get here."

"I'll make Jigsaw a very wet bran mash with salts in it; that may help," I suggested.

"How many oats has he been having and for how long?" asked Ben.

"Half a bucket, twice a day," said Lisa.

"Oh . . ." shouted Ben and used words we

are definitely not allowed to use. "No wonder he's sweating and in agony. You're a horrid little fiend, Lisa."

"Even when he's working, he doesn't need that amount," I cried. "You must be crazy."

"We had better not give Broncho too much either," said Ben. "Let's pick him out some good hay."

At three o'clock we rang up our vet who is called Roy, and he arrived at four, walking from the crossroads carrying his bag.

"So he really *did* come from Coventry," he said, looking at Broncho. "I thought you were joking when you telephoned."

"He's ill, isn't he?" I asked. "He must be. Do you think he will ever be well again? Look at his breathing for a start."

"Actually, considering everything, he looks in remarkably good condition," said Roy, shaking his stethoscope.

"He's not fit to travel, anyway," I suggested.

"Obviously not for a day or two," answered Roy, listening to Broncho's breathing while I held his head. "But his chest is clear and in a few days he'll be almost his old self," he finished.

My heart was in my boots now. "Let's look at Jigsaw, then," I said.

He gave Jigsaw an injection while Lisa watched him, tense and distraught. "Nothing but meadow hay, no clover, please," he said, shutting his bag, "and as soon as possible quiet walking exercise. I'll call again the day after tomorrow unless you ring me. And don't worry about the liver chestnut, he's going to be all right."

We said, "Thank you very much," and watched him go.

"So that is that," exclaimed Ben. "It's back to Coventry for Hillingdon Prince esquire and there's not a thing we can do."

"Have you noticed a warm air stream?" asked James, appearing from the direction of the house. "Look at the weather cock on the stable. The wind is changing, it's moving to the southwest and listen – things are dripping."

"It's the gutters," said Ben.

"Just at the wrong time," I answered.

"Why are you so glum?" asked James.

"Because it means Broncho can go," I said.

Then at six o'clock Jean Nuttal rang. "The film company want him back," she said. "So I'll send a box for him as soon as the weather clears. It's not fair that you should have all of the expense, and really he isn't your responsibility, dear."

"He won't box," I said.

"Perhaps you can ride over. I'll pay you for it, dear," she said.

And there was no answer to that.

"It's thawing," she continued, "And the roads are clear here; thanks to the snow ploughs and salt. Could you bring him over in three days' time?"

"If the roads are clear," I said.

"You are a dear. Thank you. It's so lovely

that he's safe and sound, isn't it? You must tell me all about it when you come. Goodbye for now, dear . . ."

"That's that, then. She wants him back in three days," I said.

I prayed for rain, but the weather forecast announced a thaw right across the country. The fields and yard became a sea of sludge. The roads ran with melting snow. The sun shone. Suddenly we had spring in January.

"Just our luck," I said.

Broncho improved every hour. I listened hopefully for breathing difficulties and looked for swollen joints, for anything which would delay his going but without success. Jigsaw made good progress too. Roy came again and marvelled at Broncho and announced Jigsaw cured, subject to sensible feeding, and slow exercise. "We caught it in good time," he said.

The sun shone. Snowdrops forced their way through the last of the snow.

And then the day came to take Broncho to Mrs Nuttal's, a distance of some eight miles. "I'll come with you," said Lisa. "I'll ride Lorraine and lead Jigsaw. He'll be better with company."

Mummy packed us sandwiches, though we had been promised lunch by Jean Nuttal. "Ring up when you get there," she said. "Otherwise I shall worry the whole day long."

"I wish I was coming with you," said Ben, seeing us off in the stable yard.

There was still snow on the hills, so we had to ride all the way by road. Broncho felt bouncy and alert, Lorraine jogged. It was a lovely day for a ride – an April day in January.

Yet, as I rode, it was as though my heart was breaking. I am betraying Broncho again, I thought. And he's been through so much to come home. But as Dad said, one must keep to the law of the land and that law made it possible for people to own animals, and the film company owned Broncho.

As for him, he walked with a swinging walk, little knowing what awaited him, and that made it worse. If he could have talked I could have told him, explained. As it was, there was nothing I could say which could make him understand.

And the sunshine made it worse, for the day was too lovely for sorrow. Mummy called the weather a gift straight from heaven, and it was in a way, after the snow.

And every time I looked at Lisa she was crying, and that didn't help at all! The roads were full of cars and lorries travelling too fast, as though trying to make up for the time when they couldn't travel at all.

We rode for two hours and then we could see Mrs Nuttal's place which was called Badger's End. Broncho raised his head and sniffed the air and we could see a stable yard of modern loose boxes, and two plump dogs lying in the sun. We had eaten our sandwiches at eleven o'clock but we were hungry again.

Jean Nuttal appeared from the house and waved. The dogs came to life and barked. Horses raised their heads and neighed, foals pushed their noses upwards, desperately trying to see over loose box doors.

We dismounted and Jean Nuttal, patting Broncho said, "Yes, he does look a bit poorly, doesn't he? But all to the good, he won't be able to put up such a fight when he gets back."

"When are they coming for him?" I asked.

"Not for a few days. Put him in the loose box over there and shut the top door; we don't want to lose him again, do we?" she said.

Lisa put Lorraine and Jigsaw into empty loose boxes, which had hay and water ready, and then we wandered indoors and told Jean Nuttal about Broncho's rescue, as she cooked us omelettes. The house was full of sporting prints and photographs of Broncho's relations, with champion rosettes pinned to their bridles.

When I had finished Mrs Nuttal said, "Well, I think you've all been marvellous, dear. Now sit down and eat before it's cold."

And I thought, she'll never understand how awful it was, nobody will. Then Lisa asked a very sensible question. "Can you tell us why Broncho has been so difficult? I mean all his relations look all right. What happened?"

And Mrs Nuttal said, "It's a long story but

simple too. It all began with my back, it went bad on me. Usually I break my young horses myself, all by kindness, but my back was agony and Hillingdon Prince was a strong young horse and I just hadn't the strength to cope. So I did something I had never done before, I sent him away to be broken."

"Before you sent him to us?" I asked.

"Yes, that's right. I sent him to a man called Jim Chapman for three weeks at fifty pounds a week."

"And what happened?" cried Lisa.

"He put a dumb jockey on him. Do you know what it is?"

"I think so."

"A terrible contraption which runs from the bit to the back and puts the horse's head in an overbent position and keeps it there. Of course if I had known he had one, nothing on earth would have persuaded me to let him touch Broncho," she said.

"And how long did he leave it on?" I asked, seeing it all in my mind's eye. Broncho's back aching, his hocks, his neck.

"This is the worst part of it," replied Jean Nuttal. "He put it on meaning to come back in half an hour, but he crashed his car and didn't get back until next day . . ."

"Didn't he have any help?" I asked.

"No, he lives alone."

"Couldn't he have sent anyone?" asked Lisa, beginning to sniff.

"He was unconscious."

"So Broncho stood all night with his head

strapped in one position?" I asked just to be sure.

"Yes. And after that he wouldn't let anyone touch his back, not until you had him," said Jean Nuttal.

"Which explains why he went mad when the trainer at the film place put side reins on him – he thought they were going to be on all night," I cried.

"I expect so, dear." Jean Nuttal was opening a tin of fruit now.

"It's so sad," said Lisa.

"It's worse than that," I answered. "It explains everything. Poor little horse. I never thought he was a rogue. It must have been agony – torture. Think how his neck must have ached, and his back. I can't bear to think about it."

"But he was always strong," said Mrs Nuttal, handing me a bowl of tinned peaches. "Even as a foal, he knew where he was going. His dam was the same. Whatever happened, he would have been a handful."

"Have you told the film company about his background?" I asked. "Because it is important, isn't it? He's got to trust them and I have a feeling he doesn't trust men after what happened to him."

"I will," replied Mrs Nuttal.

"He knew I wasn't a dumb jockey," said Lisa.

"He may have felt safer without a bridle," I answered.

And now everything seemed over. We

understood Broncho, too late, of course, but at least we now knew the reason for his fear.

After lunch I said goodbye to Broncho and then I locked him back in his prison and rode away with the sound of his despairing neighs in my ears.

I felt very cold and very sad, as though someone I had loved was dead and Lisa's small face looked pinched with despair. We didn't talk, because we knew that words were now incapable of altering anything. We rode very fast; but it was still dusk when we reached home. There was a crowd waiting for us in the stable yard.

"What happened?" cried Mummy.

"Nothing."

"You promised to telephone."

"We forgot," I answered. "Why didn't you ring Mrs Nuttal?"

"We did but she didn't answer," replied Mummy. "We were about to send out a search party."

"I'm sorry," I slid to the ground realizing for the first time how small and ponyish Lorraine was after Hillingdon Prince.

"It's back to school again tomorrow," said Mummy. "The roads are quite clear now."

And so, I thought, the chapter's ended. Broncho, Hillingdon Prince, whatever you call him, goes back to his owners and this time they will be more careful. And I go back to school.

Mike had cleaned out the boxes for us and put everything ready. The lights from the house glimmered in the dusk. "We've got a granny and three children coming at Easter," said Mummy. And so, I thought, in spite of everything, life goes on. We are back to the old routine. But I was wrong.

# Twelve
## Proper contracts

I dreamed that Broncho was in the yard and that I was locked in my room, unable to get out. I could hear the clatter of buckets and Cassie's welcoming neigh but my door was bolted and the window barred. And then suddenly I realized that it wasn't a dream, but real. I leapt out of bed and rushed to my window. The yard was full of moonlight and Broncho really was wandering about pushing his nose into buckets. I pulled on a sweater and trousers and rushed downstairs and I found my boots. I bumped into Lisa in the kitchen.

"Broncho's back," she cried.

"Yes, I know," I shouted.

I fell on the garden path because the slush had frozen. When I reached the yard, Broncho raised a bedraggled head and whinnied. I opened his box door and he went inside.

"You don't belong here," I said. "You're not ours any more. Can't you understand?" He looked in the manger and nuzzled my pockets. He looked pleased with himself, and then I saw that one of his legs was soaked in blood. "You are a fool," I said. "What have you done now?" I leant down to look and he nuzzled my hair.

Lisa was staring over the box door now.

"We need antiseptic and cotton wool. He must have broken his loose box door down," I said.

His chest was covered with scratches and one of his eyes was half closed, but it didn't seem to worry him; he was obviously delighted to be home. We bathed his leg and fetched him hay and water and Mummy appeared and inquired, "What's happening?"

And I said, "Broncho's back."

"He seems wedded to this place. How far has he travelled this time?" she asked.

"Only eight miles," I answered, sponging his injured eye with cold water.

"He really trusts you, Harriet," Mummy said.

"He's like a faithful hound, he always comes home," I answered.

When he was settled, we drank mugs of tea in the kitchen leaning against the Aga because the central heating was off.

"I wonder what Jean Nuttal will say this time," said Lisa.

"I'm not taking him back again," I replied.

"She needs a cage with a mesh roof, to keep him in," said Mummy laughing.

It was nearly morning now, so we didn't go back to bed. Later Ben came down and at seven o'clock we telephoned Jean Nuttal. She sounded sleepy and rather cross. "I never heard a thing. Are you sure it's Prince?" she asked when I told her my news.

"Yes, without a doubt. He's pretty cut up. Has he had a tetanus injection, or will he need one?"

"No. He had a combined one – tetanus and equine flu vaccine six months ago. What are we going to do now?" she asked.

"I don't know," I said.

"I had better ring the film company. They can collect him from you this time. I don't want all my boxes smashed up. I can see his box now; the whole front is down, not just the door. It will cost a mint of money to repair. Drat the horse," she said.

"When will they come for him?" I asked.

"I'll tell them to ring you. They can pay you for keeping him in the meantime, it's only fair," replied Jean Nuttal.

A second later she rang off.

"The film company will telephone. Can't we miss school today, Mummy, please?" I cried. "Because they won't be able to box him."

"Certainly not, it's Saturday tomorrow. They can come then. Now get ready, your shoes need cleaning and your blazer's covered with horse hair."

In spite of getting up early, we all missed the bus and Mummy had to take us to school in the car, complaining loudly.

"It's not every day Broncho, sorry Hillingdon Prince, comes back," I said.

"It seems like it, though," replied Mummy.

I couldn't concentrate at school and fell asleep in maths. Finally I was sent to see the headmaster, Mr Chivers, who is bald with an egg-shaped head and goggly eyes behind glasses. He made a great many tut-tutting noises, while I explained that I had been wakened by a horse returning home. He was not amused, because nothing ever amuses Mr Chivers. He told me that I would never pass my GCSEs and that frivolity wouldn't find me a job in life and did I know that there were scores of unemployed school-leavers?

I said, "Sure, but I have a job already. I school horses." And he looked furious and answered, "Now go back to your classroom and behave in future or I shall have to see your parents and you wouldn't like that, would you?" So I said, "No." The rest of the day passed at a snail's pace. I kept imagining Broncho being taken away when I should have been drawing plants. And my exercise books became covered with his head instead of facts and figures. When at last it was time to rush outside to get into the bus, I found Ben waving with his good arm. "Mum's come for us," he yelled. "The film people have turned up."

"Already?" I said.

"I'm afraid so."

"Couldn't they have waited?" I cried, breaking into a run. "They are like vultures, aren't they? They want their pound of flesh."

"Not a pound, two thousand pounds," replied Ben.

"Two thousand, then. I wish the Trippets had never come," I said.

Mummy was wearing her best coat and high-heeled shoes.

"I suppose it's the girls with the horse box again," I said, getting into the car.

"No. It's two charming men," replied Mummy. "They are waiting for you. They won't budge from the yard until you come. They won't even have a mug of tea in the kitchen."

"Are they taking Broncho on the roof rack, then?" I asked.

"They want to talk to you. So try and be pleasant, please," Mummy answered.

"They are only prolonging the agony," I replied. "Are they waiting until they've built a cage for Broncho? I suppose that's it; they haven't got his prison ready yet."

"You're not going to blubber, are you?" asked Ben.

"Shut up," I said.

The yard was full of winter sunshine. An elegant Mercedes was parked in front of our old-fashioned tack room, which still has the fireplace before which a groom once sat, boiling kettles for fomentations and bran mashes – or so I like to think.

The men were not as I had expected. One was dressed in riding clothes, the other wore a denim suit over a polo-necked sweater. He had brown eyes and dark curly hair, which kept flopping forward. Lisa was admiring them from a distance.

"Harriet," said the one in denims, holding out his hand. "I'm Mike Mitchells." And I heard Ben give a small gasp and I thought, he must be famous.

Mummy said, "Will you come inside and have some tea? It really is teatime now." And they said, "Thanks a million. Your other daughter has been showing us around. I hope you don't mind."

"Not at all," replied Mummy, leading the way to the front door which we never normally use.

"Harry here is the horse expert. I'm just the producer," said Michael Mitchells as we crossed the hall, "I'm sorry you've had so much trouble with the horse. Gordon Trippet is one of our scouts and he thought he had spotted a winner, but he forgot temperament."

"When are you taking him away?" I asked in a voice which was meant to be cool, calm and collected but which came out with a croak in it.

"That is what we want to discuss," replied Harry.

"He isn't fit to travel," I said.

"Well, actually we don't want him to travel," replied Mike Mitchells with a smile.

"You're going to kill him, aren't you?" asked Lisa, suddenly white and tense.

"No, darling," replied Mike Mitchells, "We're not vicious. We want him to stay here. We want your big sister to train him, for which we will pay her and, subject to one or two things, we want to make the film here; we've been looking for a location and this is it. It's perfect, absolutely right, down to the last detail."

"Here?" cried Ben. "You mean actually here, in this house?"

"Yes, and in the stables. We'll have to build the odd arch, of course, for the coaches coming in and out."

"Coaches? You mean drawn by horses?" cried Lisa.

"That's right."

"Oh God!" cried James. "You don't mean it." Mummy had been listening from the kitchen; now her hand was shaking so much she spilt milk on the best sitting room carpet. "You'll have to move the guests out, of course," continued Mike Mitchells.

"When will it be?" asked Ben.

"End of May, beginning of June. We usually pay not less than five hundred pounds a day for a property like this and it could take a month."

I thought Mummy was going to faint.

"In the meantime, I want you, Harriet, to train Prince – he's going to be called that in the story, so stick to it, please," he continued. "He must be able to pass anything, particularly trains. And he must be able to swim across a river. Can you do it, Harriet?"

"Yes," I said firmly.

"He must learn to carry a sidesaddle and you may have to stand in for Miss Edwards once or twice . . ."

"You don't mean Julie Edwards?" asked Ben.

"That's right."

"Oh my God," cried James again.

"We'll draw up a proper contract, of course, and more people will have to come down to sort out the house. The staircase is perfect but we may have to alter the front gates. Do you think your husband will mind, Mrs Pemberton? We need a wide sweep to the front door and pillars."

"Definitely not," replied Mummy, sipping tea. "We never did like the gates, anyway."

"And we'll be bringing in things like period beds. If you have to move out we'll pay any hotel bills. We will need the old stables, so some of your horses will have to be moved."

"No problem there," said Ben.

"We'll draw up proper contracts and let you have them in a few days," said Mr Mitchells. "This place should look perfect by May, but we will be planting extra flowers; it will be in the contract . . ."

They were going now. I wanted to throw my arms round their necks, to shriek with joy. "Prince has done us a good turn. I would never have seen this place otherwise; it's so unspoilt," said Mike Mitchells, stepping outside and smelling the air. "It hasn't been tarted up. And the atmosphere is just right. I knew it the moment I got out of the car. It's the right period too. It really is a lovely old place."

"He's famous," cried Ben as they drove away.

"So is Julie Edwards," added James.

"I thought I was going to pass out," exclaimed Mummy.

"How shall I teach Broncho to swim, I mean Prince," I asked.

"And you are going to be paid," cried James. "You're so lucky."

"I feel sick," said Lisa.

"And here comes Dad," shouted Ben, and we started to dance and shout like lunatics. "Everything is all right," I screamed.

"We're going to be rich," yelled Ben.

"Just wait until you hear," said James.

I thought, I shall never have time for two horses. "You can have Lorraine now, Lisa," I said. "You're big enough, and I'm too big. Okay?"

"Okay," she said. "And I'll lend Jigsaw to Rosie. She'll pay us to keep him and she does need a pony desperately. And she's my best friend at school."

So suddenly all the cold and the agony seemed worthwhile.

"We're made," said Dad when at last everyone had stopped talking. "We can advertise Black Pony Inn as the house used in such-and-such a film. People will come in droves, we'll never be half empty again."

"We must celebrate," said Mummy. "Steve and Janet have just left and Colonel Hunter loves a celebration."

"We must do the horses first," I said. "After

all, it began with them, didn't it? Because if it hadn't been for Broncho, I mean Prince . . ."

"But what about the Trippets? We hated them but look what's happened!" said James.

"I don't know where it began or where it will end but it's wonderful just the same," cried Mummy, putting her arm through Dad's. "Let's all go out. Let's blow Steve's money. He paid in cash. I'm sick to death of cooking. Let's have a super-duper dinner at The Old White Lion."

"But who owns Broncho – I mean Prince – now?" cried Lisa.

"Them, I suppose," I said. "But he's going to stay here and who knows what may happen between now and the end of the filming?"

"We may all be film stars," shouted Lisa.

"Colonel Hunter will have to move out," said Dad. "Now get on and wash. I don't want you all smelling of horse at The Old White Lion."

We chose what we wanted for dinner, and the dining room was lit by candles and was full of people in evening dress. The waiters were Spanish and wore red and white rugger shirts. We were all a bit tatty in appearance except for Colonel Hunter who came too and wore a dinner jacket.

Three days later a fat envelope came from the film company containing two contracts, one concerning the house and one concerning Prince, as we now called him. Prince's had my name at the top. It was very long and full of terms like "vested interests" which I didn't understand. But the gist of it was something like this: Hillingdon Prince remained the property of the film company until he was of no further use to them when he became mine. He had to reside with me but I had to agree to let them use him at any given time for filming, them being responsible for my travelling expenses and his, and a daily fee for any time I spent on location, the exact sum yet to be decided. I would also receive an outright fee of four hundred pounds for schooling him, and a fee of forty pounds a week for his keep as long as he was with us. (This would, of course, cease when he became my property.) I would also be required to swim a river on Prince and perform some of the parts Julie Edwards couldn't (made up to look like her, of course) for which I would be paid.

It was the most exciting letter I had ever received. Dad was equally pleased with the contract concerning the house.

And best of all, Prince would now be with us forever, a Prince at Black Pony Inn, insured against injury, mine as he grew older, a horse in a thousand to grace our stables. So suddenly the future looked brighter than the brightest day. And May glowed in the distance, a magic month when Julie Edwards would come to act out a script in our ancient house, and Prince would make his debut as a film star.

We walked about in a dream. All our troubles suddenly over. Our happiness seeming to stretch to eternity and now, at last, money didn't matter any more.